The Letter BOMB

Based on a True Story

BY STEVEN M. JONES

DORRANCE
PUBLISHING CO
EST. 1920
PITTSBURGH, PENNSYLVANIA 15238

Dorrance Publishing Co
585 Alpha Drive
Suite 103
Pittsburgh, PA 15238
Visit our website at *www.dorrancebookstore.com*

ISBN: 979-8-88729-479-7
eISBN: 979-8-88729-979-2

The Letter BOMB

Based on a True Story

DRAFT – PRIVATE & CONFIDENTIAL

Dear U.S. Senate Foreign Relations Committee,

Patrium was formed in 1992 with the signing of the Schonbrunn Peace Treaty coming after the fall of the Berlin Wall in 1989, and the complete dissolution of the former Union of Soviet Socialist Republics (USSR) in 1991. Under the terms and conditions in the Schonbrunn Peace Treaty, pieces of several formerly Soviet satellite countries were reassembled into one new nation – Patrium – created to become a safe, democratic, and independent haven for well over one million refugees from all over the European continent. In Latin, Patrium means "homeland." Patrium's leaders were chosen in a free and open election process that was carefully monitored and validated by the United Nations.

As a new nation Patrium is desperately in need of new ideas and technologies that can expand our economy and foster economic growth. The support of the United States of America (USA) is vital to Patrium's success in achieving these objectives.

Patrium has applied for admission to the North Atlantic Treaty Organization (NATO). To demonstrate our commitment to joining NATO we are currently spending over 2% of our GDP on purchasing defense-related products and services that meet or exceed NATO requirements. Most of these products and services are made in the USA.

Over the last several years working in Patrium for Alkodomo Trading Company, Mr. Wallace B. "Biff" Child has generated pre-award industrial cooperation/offset credits that *exceed 500%* of the anticipated Contract Award Value for Patrium's acquisition of previously owned and operated United States Air Force (USAF) F-16 and C-130 aircraft. Our offset requirement is 100% of the Contract Award value for all defense acquisitions.

In recognition of this remarkable achievement, we the undersigned respectively request that the U.S. Senate Foreign Relations Committee consider Wallace B. "Biff" Child as a future United States Ambassador to the nation of Patrium.

Sincerely,

PROLOGUE

If you're looking for a fun and adventurous "Huck Finn" story about an average kid's life growing up in America in the fifties and sixties, about bullies and braggarts, about loving family and friends, about love at first sight, about the heartland of America, about muscle cars and custom paint jobs, about the business of selling U.S. military aircraft to international allies, about being the scapegoat of a national scandal, and the existential battle of good versus evil, then you've come to the right place.

This is a work of fiction based on a true story. Any similarity to actual persons, living or dead, or actual events, is purely coincidental.

Steven M. Jones

Dedication

This book is dedicated to:

My wife, who inspired it; my daughters, their husbands, and my grandchildren.

My mom and dad, sisters, cousins, best friends, and my entire extended family.

The people of Mitchell, Indiana and to Spring Mill State Park.

Mark Twain and Will Rogers, my two favorite American authors and humorists.

Thank you to Wikipedia for providing general background information and facts.

TABLE OF CONTENTS

PREFACE – PHOTO GALLERY

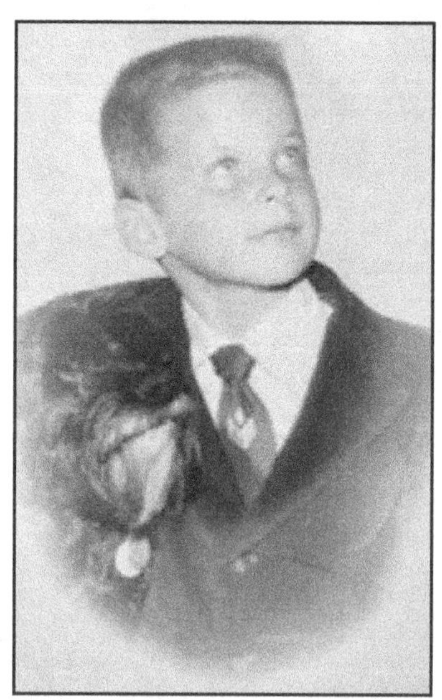

Bathing Beach, Spring Mill State Park, Mitchell, Indiana

Games Scenes at U.C.L.A.

Olympic Gold Medalist Greg Louganis

1968 Plymouth Barracuda

1969 Plymouth Roadrunner

1968 Dodge Charger

Bob's

CHAPTER ONE

BIFF'S BOYHOOD IN 1950'S AND 1960'S AMERICANA

I was born in 1950 in a small, south-central Indiana town named Mitchell at 421 Warren Street, across from the fire station. Mitchell had about 3,500 people at the time, and was best known for building Carpenter school buses and its large Lehigh Cement Plant. It was famous to my family because Bill, my dad, was the center on the *only* Mitchell High School basketball team (1940) that *ever* went to the state finals in the history of the town. Mitchell High School lost the game, but nonetheless made the local history books. Dad went on to become a Little All-American basketball player for Georgetown College in Kentucky.

Spring Mill State Park is a 1,358-acre state park located about three miles outside of Mitchell. It contains a magnificent old-fashioned inn tucked into a lush hardwood forest, the historic astronaut Virgil 'Gus' Grissom Memorial, a rich nature center, expansive, well-equipped campgrounds, miles of hiking trails, deep dark caves, a swimming pool for the whole family, and a pioneer village. The water flowing from several cave springs led to the founding of the pioneer village in the early 1800s. Pioneer entrepreneurs took advantage of a constant water source that never froze, using it to power several gristmills, a wool mill, a saw mill, and a distillery. In turn, pioneer settlers shaped the landscape around the village, clearing land for agriculture and timber.

In the 1960s, before the swimming pool was installed, the park had a "bathing beach" with a snack bar that led down a dozen concrete stairs to a swimming area carved out of the icy cold, spring-fed lake. An area about a hundred yards wide that could safely contain about 2,000 people was roped off around a man-made sandy beach. I was a lifeguard on this beach along with four other guys for the summers of 1965, 1966, and 1967. Over the three summers I can still remember Dunbar, Eversole, Stroud, Henderson, Baugh, and Blunt. Somebody had a "bitchin" Mustang GT that was fast, loud, and cool in black with four on the floor.

One July 4th, always our busiest day of the summer, we counted over 3,000 people spread between the recreation center, beach, and in the water! That day, an elderly woman had an epileptic seizure right on the center of the beach and was swallowing her tongue. An Indiana University medical student standing nearby yelled, "Grab her tongue! Grab her tongue!"

In my role as a lifeguard, I tried to grab her tongue with two popsicle sticks and a piece of cloth somebody shoved into my hands while two other lifeguards held her steady during her seizure.

That failing, the medical student grabbed a huge diaper pin from a nearby lady's diaper bag and thrust it into my hand. "Stick it through her tongue and hold on! If she swallows her tongue, she'll choke to death before the ambulance gets here!"

I stuck it through her tongue and held on. The two other lifeguards held on to her as strongly and gently as they could. It seemed like forever for the ambulance to get there, coming from Bedford over ten miles away. Get there it did, and the paramedics took it from there, saving her life. In that moment, for the first time, it hit all five of us like a ton of bricks how serious our lifeguard jobs really were.

Three tall, steel lifeguard chairs were installed—two on the beach and one on the concrete pier permanently anchored about fifty feet from the beach. A wooden diving board was installed and anchored to the pier; it was so loosely fitted you had to jump up and down on the end of the diving board several times to get enough height to do a one and a half properly! Two steel ladders led out of the water onto the pier on either side of the diving board. The pier was where all the teenagers wanted to hang out, "shoot the breeze," and maybe take a dive or two if they weren't afraid to mess up their hair.

For a young boy growing up in the 1950s, Mitchell was like heaven on earth. Our house on Warren Street was a stone's throw from the railroad tracks (Mitchell was a crossroads for the B&O and Monon railroads). Every summer night I would run down to the tracks when the train whistle blew, catch a firefly or two on the way in a Mason jar to admire, and then let it go and put a penny on the tracks so the train would squash it and turn into a squished lucky penny! As a typical American boy in Indiana, I got my own bright red Schwinn bike, Red Ryder BB rifle and hand gun, red imperial Duncan yo-yo, slingshot, Davy Crockett/Daniel Boone rifle–powder horn–raccoon skin cap, Voit football and basketball, Rawling's baseball and baseball glove with the sixth finger for us outfielders, Hutch catcher's mitt, and a Black Beauty bat with Duke Snider's signature on it! I could go on and on but, man, I was "walking in tall cotton" and didn't even know it, or care! Life was a dream in the summer. Play outside all morning, come back for lunch to grab a peanut butter and jelly sandwich on Wonder Bread with a Claussen pickle and a Big Red, and then right back outside!

Every scratch or bruise could be fixed with Merthiolate. Every cough or cold with Vick's VapoRub. Every pulled muscle with Bengay. If a bone wasn't broken and sticking out of your skin, the best you would get was, "Walk it off, kid!" Play, play, play until just before six P.M., hose yourself off with the garden hose before going in the house, and be sitting in your seat at the kitchen nook at exactly six P.M. sharp or no supper for you, and a whoopin' to go with it! You even got to cut your own switch off the peach tree for your whoopin'. Too big, it hurt like the dickens. Too small, you had to go cut another one and got one more lick for trying to be sneaky.

My big sister, Allison, was one year older than me. She reminded me of Sophia Loren—tall, voluptuous, and beautiful. She was totally sweet and kindhearted. My middle sister, Marcella, was one year younger than me. She reminded me of Farrah Fawcett—sexy, mysterious, tough, and vivacious; also "ornery as a striped-ass snake" as they said in Indiana, with fingernails that could rip the flesh off your arm with one flick of her wrist. My baby sister, Anne, was two years younger than me. She was tall and blond with a constantly sunny disposition. She reminded me of Athena, the Greek goddess of music. Anne was a gifted cellist who studied under world-renowned Spanish cellist, Pablo Casals. To round out the family later in life, Allison would marry Tim;

Marcella would marry Alan; Anne would marry Mark, and Keta-Kot would marry Tim; all became my "Bro-Mo's"–brothers of a different mother.

For meals, we four kids sat in the kitchen on a rounded vinyl bench in the nook. Mom and Dad had stand-alone chairs. No talking or kibitzing allowed! Mom had a set menu for the week that I loved. Kraft macaroni and cheese with sliced hot dogs on Monday, chipped beef with white gravy on Tuesday (that my dad called "shit on a shingle" from his Navy days), white beans with ham chunks in it and cornbread on Wednesday, hamburger patties with peas and pearl onions on Thursday (how I hated those slimy eye-ball looking pearl onions), and fish sticks with green beans on Friday. On the weekends, Mom "played it by ear." If we didn't like something, Mom had put on our Melmac plate, we did our best to wrap it in a napkin and secretly pass it to another sibling who liked it, an almost perfect familial barter system.

After teaching school, putting together Blue Chip and S&H stamp savings books, doing the laundry, and making sure I'd watered the front lawn to the proper depth, Mom's mind was going a mile a minute at dinnertime. She didn't have a clue about our secret system, so Dad was the only one we had to keep our eyes peeled for. If he caught us, we knew we would surely get a swat from the infamous "Georgetown paddle," Dad's fraternity paddle from his college days. If nobody wanted your contraband (and I couldn't stand those pearly white "eyeball" onions that came in the pea can), you had two choices: feed it to our dog Ghia, or push it all the way down behind the bench seat couch cushion.

Ghia was a black and white spaniel with long, floppy ears. She loved to drink out of the toilet, then come out into the living room and flap her wet, toilet-water ears all over everybody–which my dad absolutely hated sitting on his usual place in the curve of the sofa. How dare she interrupt *Bonanza*, or the *Ed Sullivan Show*, or a golf tournament, showering him with vaporized toilet water and foamy saliva! Ghia was one of the sweetest dogs we ever owned, and us kids huddled over her and protected her no matter what she did.

If Ghia actually took what you gave her and swallowed it, you were home free. However, if she gagged on it and noisily spit it out, you were dead meat and going to get the Georgetown after supper; no questions asked. When I got caught, Dad always spanked me with the Georgetown squarely on my "cheeks," one swat, hard enough to sting but not hard enough to hurt, and then off I'd go back outside to play baseball with my best buddy, LK, until it got dark and the mosquitos came out. I don't know why my Type AB+ blood was so attractive to mosquitos, but I imagined them having a tiny triangle like the cowboys had that the Wagon Train cook used to *clang* to signal suppertime to the cowboys. Those "skeeters" came after me like bad on ugly as soon as the sun set. I could be standing in the middle of my sisters or friends and I was the only one being attacked. "Why me, God? Why me?"

Dad did very little cooking, but he did have his specialties. There was always a small tub of bacon grease in the refrigerator, an Indiana tradition. He used it to make popcorn in his old black skillet with a stainless-steel lid, and we loved it. LK ate more of it than any of us which was, of course, verboten for a Jewish child preparing for his bar mitzvah. Dad used it to make fried eggs and cook yellow corn squash on Saturday mornings which I never missed. Keta-Kot carried on the tradition whenever she and Tim visited us from Indiana. Then on Saturday night, Dad took me, just me, snackin' shoppin' at the Piggly Wiggly grocery store where he dug into the recesses of his wallet to pull out the neatly folded and well-hidden twenty-dollar-emergency-bill to buy me a box of Cracker Jacks.

If you did something wrong in the neighborhood, you knew some nosey neighbor would tell on you and you were gonna get punished. "It takes a village to raise a child." Geez Louis, a bunch of rat finks! The good news was my punishment was always swift, safe, and sure, and then off I'd go. My parents knew the worst thing they could do to me was ground me in my room and keep me from going outside. Under threat of confinement in my bedroom by myself, I got pretty good at following the daily reminder to "Just behave and fly right!"

School was school. Boring except for recess on the playground and after-school sports. Sherman Oaks Junior High School and Sherman Oaks High School looked like all the schools you see on TV—dark beige with olive green wood trim borders; the perfect muted colors for locking up prisoners against their will for eight hours a day! Actually, both campuses were well-kept and had lots of shade trees, but it was still prison to us kids.

In Grade B9 (the final year of junior high) school I decided to ditch my 'dad's flat-top haircut and let my hair grow longer. As it was growing out, I looked like I'd stuck my finger in a wall socket with hair going in every direction. Holey Moley, this would never work! I got some "butch wax," hair wax that was like axle grease, and plastered it on my hair. Still some stragglers sticking up. That night I wore one of my sisters' discarded stockings on my head with cut-outs for my eyes, nose, and mouth. It worked! The next day my hair looked perfect, just in time for school pictures.

That same semester a new kid, Mike, transferred into our school and grade. He was quick to tell everybody he knew karate, so stay out of his way! He asked one of my buddies who the toughest kid in B9 was, and like an idiot my buddy said, "Biff."

The next thing I knew, this new kid I didn't even know and hadn't spoken to was in my face "choosing me off" for a fight on the B9 lawn after school at three o'clock.

I was no chicken, and had no clue what was going on, but I said, "Okay."

At three o'clock, we squared off on the B9 lawn with a whole bunch of kids circled around to hide the fight from the nearby teachers, vice principal, and principal. Mike jumped into his karate pose. I leaped forward and punched him in the nose as hard as I could, just like my dad had taught me.

"Son, avoid a fight if you can, try to talk your way out of it. If you can't talk your way out of it, and can't or won't walk away, throw the first punch, and hit the guy right smack in the nose as hard as you can. His eyes will water up instantly and he won't be able to see anyone or anything for a minute or two. Hopefully, the other kids will jump in and break up the fight and nobody will get badly hurt."

I can count the father/son talks I had with my dad on one hand. One of them was *not* the "birds and the bees." This advice from Dad spared me from getting the dickens knocked out of me by bullies and loud-mouths *many* times in my life. I never lost a fight using his technique since I was fast and strong.

Grade A9 was the top of the heap in junior high school. We had our own "A9 lawn" that no student below A9 could even step on or they got beat up and chased off. I took trigonometry in A9 from a teacher we called "Twitch" because he had a nervous tick on his face every time he got upset with any one of us.

"Trig" was hard, you had to study to pass, and I hated it. My buddies and I used to pass notes back and forth and whisper across the aisle which apparently made Twitch very irritated. I sat three chairs from the back in the second row from the wall. One day, while whispering across the aisle to my buddy, I felt a gust of air whoosh past my head. I instantly looked up and around, and two seats behind me against the back wall my baseball buddy, Big O., was looking down on the floor at an eraser Twitch had thrown at me! I didn't know it was thrown at me until Twitch looked directly at me from the front of the class and yelled, "Pick it up!"

My temper instantly flared and I snarled back, "*You* threw it; *you* pick it up!"

You could have heard a pin drop, a "Mexican stand-off" between a teacher and a student was unheard of in the annals of Sherman Oaks Junior High. Big O. picked up the eraser and brought it to Twitch. Twitch went back to teaching acting as if nothing had happened. Above my waist, I had my macho "I showed him!" tough guy look on my face. Under my desk, my knees were banging together like two giant cymbals in the orchestra. My mom was a teacher for goodness' sake! She would never take my side in a million years. I envisioned myself being dragged to Juvenile Hall, or maybe prison! I put my head way down and whispered across to my buddy, "This guy is crazy!"

A second later, another eraser whizzed past my head and hit the back wall. Same demand, same response—on with class he went. Now my legs were banging together uncontrollably. Head down again, I whispered the same words to my buddy across the aisle, when *whammo* I got hit in the forehead with a third eraser! My buddy told me later Twitch had tip-toed down the aisle, gotten three feet away, and threw the eraser at me as hard as he could. Then he tip-toed back to the front of the class and turned around with a big grin on his face. I brushed the chalk dust off my face and eyes, picked up the eraser on my desk right in front of me, and waited for him to turn around. As soon as he did, I used my left fielder's arm to throw the eraser and plug him right in the chest from the back of the room.

He acted like I'd hit him with a brick, stumbled over to the front doorway frame, and twitched wildly with his head hung low. Stony silence filled the room for what seemed like an eternity. Then the recess bell rang, and we all ran out of the room like it was a fire drill. I raced to the quad where I knew the Boys VP would be like he was every day, and blurted out my story, using a make-believe "what if a teacher did this, and what if a student did that?" scenario.

He laughed and said, "That teacher would be in a *lot* of trouble!"

Yeah, that's what I thought! That's what I'd tell my mom when she got the call from the school. I swaggered around with my head held high for the rest of the day. News spread through the school like wildfire. I was an instant celebrity; the guy who stood up to the teacher. I was larger than life for the rest of my junior high school career because Twitch never told anybody, and my mom never got the dreaded call. Unfortunately, Twitch gave me a well-deserved D grade which was still "barely passing" on my report card. I didn't have to take trig again because a D is barely passing–or so I thought.

The story 'didn't end there, however. When my dad saw my report card and the D grade, he hit the ceiling. He said, "You failed trigonometry, now you'll have to take it in summer school until you pass."

I calmly responded, "But, Dad, a D is barely passing, like it says in small print on the report card. I don't have to take it again."

My dad was reclining on the couch watching golf on TV, and I was twenty feet away standing against the heater wall. Like a tiger, he leaped off the couch and started toward me, right fist clenched, fire in his black-out temper eyes. It seemed like it took him a week to get from the couch to me. My mind went back to his shaking hand in the garage after he'd punched a wall in a fit of rage. I tried to decide if my head should be away from the wall, or against the wall when he punched me in my disrespectful mouth. I thought about the headache I'd have after the punch. I thought about having to take trig again. He was charging and looking right at me.

At the last instant, his eyes dropped to my left shoulder, he pulled his punch, turned me around, grabbed me by my shirt collar and the seat of my pants, and gave me "flying lessons" into my bedroom ten feet away. I landed in a heap, got up, straightened my clothes, and sat down on the side of the bed awaiting further instructions. *Not so bad,* I thought to myself. I deserved much worse for appearing to talk back to him–which was, of course, verboten. I dreamed about being outside playing baseball with LK.

Five minutes later, Dad came in and barked, "I had no business doing that. I want you to punch me."

In total bewilderment, being the obedient son, I punched him in the shoulder exactly as hard as he had punched me; no more, no less; the same.

He said, "You're free to go," and walked out of the room.

At that moment in time, my respect for my dad pegged the meter.

My troubles in A9 didn't end there. One day, a bunch of us guys were play-ing street baseball in front of Big O's house like we always did on the weekend. Across the street a neighbor was putting fresh cement in a small triangle next to his driveway. When he was done, and had gone away, LR decided to leave his mark on the world and poked a stick into the fresh cement making a small hole. He beamed with pride over his tiny hole that would be there forever! I took his stick and wrote "the F-word" in small letters next to his hole just to show off. In shock, my buddies all ran away leaving me standing there next to my work of art. I ran home thinking I was in the clear.

An hour later, my dad got a call from Big O's dad telling him what I'd done. I was dragged into the car and minutes later we were at the scene of the crime. My dad apologized to the owner of the concrete triangle and promised I would pay any and all costs for fixing it out of my allowance mowing lawns and cleaning the pool next-door, which I did.

Instead of spanking me, or grounding me, or worse, he bent down and cupped my face in his hands. "Do you know what that word means?"

I said, "I do not," which I thought was a bold-faced lie, since I knew that "the F-word" really meant "boy's hand on a girl's butt."

Dad knew how immature I was, and that I didn't *really* know, so he sternly said, "You're going to pay every penny to fix that cement. That was a stupid, idiotic, and inconsiderate thing to do. Never do that again!"

I had no idea why he let me off the hook that easily when he had so many punishment options available. I concluded in my childlike mind he considered me like Ghia, a stupid dog that drank out of the toilet, ate its own poop, and then licked you in the face out of pure, unadulterated love. Dad never beat Ghia, and he wasn't going to beat me.

My given name was Wallace B. Child. My dad wanted the B to stand for "Baxter," but my mom always wanted it to stand for "Billy" which to her was a "cute name for a boy." To compromise, it became just plain B on my birth certificate. Mom always called me Billy, so the rest of the family respectfully followed her lead. That was fine until I got to third grade, when many young boys seem to turn into bullies and become just plain mean. That was also the year Sherman Oaks Elementary School administrators decided to skip me half a year from B3 into A3, joining a group of kids I didn't know at all; not one of them. I was short, skinny, and shy with a big Frankenstein head. I kept to myself, hoping everyone would just leave me alone. Unfortunately, fate had other plans for me.

One wise guy in my new class decided my new name should be "Billy Goat" and passed it on to all the other guys during recess on the playground. He started a group chant that got louder and louder, and soon about ten mean boys were chanting, "Billy Goat, Billy Goat, Billy Goat!"

At that very instant, I discovered I had my dad's Irish black-out temper, knocked the big-mouthed leader to the ground, bleeding profusely, with one punch to the nose my dad had taught me, and screamed at the rest of the kids, "My name is Biff!"

So where did that come from? I was a Superman comic book fan, and every time Superman punched a bad guy there were cartoon stars with the words *Biff, Bam, Pow* in them. In my childlike mind in my bedroom with nobody around, I had mentally changed my name from Billy to "Biff." Biff was afraid of nothing and no one. He believed in truth, justice, and the American way, like Superman. He watched Mighty Mouse cartoons where the opening song was "Here I come to save the day, Mighty Mouse is on the way!"

Biff came to life in a fit of rage during that fight on the playground. From that day forward, all the kids called me Biff, and all my family and teachers called me Billy.

I was labelled a "late bloomer" by my teachers because my performance didn't match my IQ. They skipped me in third grade hoping to light a fire under me and challenge me more, but it didn't work very well. The lowest grades I was allowed to receive were four A's, one B, and one C, and that's exactly what I got thanks to a big push at the end of the semester to make up for my lack of interest the first 9/10[ths] of the semester. I was easygoing and polite, so my teachers liked me; I knew from eavesdropping on my elementary school teacher Mom's conversations with other teachers that if I showed dramatic improvement at the end of the semester they would attribute it to their hard work, dedication, and skill. All I knew was my start lazy, end in a fireball strategy worked out great most of the time.

I just didn't like being in school when I could be outside playing sports. My best friend from three years old, LK and I, made up all kinds of fun outdoor games that kept us busy and out of trouble. LK lived right down the block on our cul-de-sac with his mom and dad and two older brothers. He became my best friend for life, brother of a different mother, and we hung out together every day. We never studied school stuff together; all we did was play outside if there was daylight to burn. I absolutely loved his mom, and thanked his two older brothers for their hand-me-down clothes that were much more in style than my JC Penney and Sears clothes.

LK's dad beat their Dalmatian dog almost every night across the street from of our house to force it to go to the bathroom, slapped his boys around unmercifully, and was a person I avoided like the plague. He slapped me one summer on my shirtless back and left a handprint that was still there when I got home. My dad was going to pulverize him, but my mom stopped him, fearing a lawsuit. She loved LK like a son, and still does.

"Hit the bat" was fun to play in the middle of the street on our cul-de-sac, using "bottle caps" to see who batted first (alternate hands up the bat from the fat part to the handle with the kid who didn't have room for a full hand on the handle and having to put his/her hand over the flared end of the bat declaring bottle cap). I think my parents just figured I would bloom one of these days and didn't worry about me.

They had their plateful, raising three daughters shoehorned into one bedroom with only one unlockable bathroom on our side of the house. The four of us were born one year apart, so just imagine what it was like when the girls were sixteen, fourteen, and thirteen! I felt sorry for my parents having three girls who didn't always see eye to eye when I was such a little angel playing outside all the time and keeping my bedroom tidy without hardly ever having to be nagged or spanked or punished (tongue in cheek).

The four of us got along great together, and still do. We protected each other no matter what, and never let anybody say anything bad about any of us. All for one, and one for all, just like the Three Musketeers.

Every Easter, Dad and Mom drove us to Las Vegas, Nevada to see our grammie and gramps (my mom's father and step-mother). I used to love the Burma-Shave signs along the way. Burma-Shave was an American brand of brushless shaving cream, famous for its advertising gimmick of posting humorous rhyming poems on small sequential highway roadside signs. For example, these six signs: "If you dislike/Big traffic fines/Slow down/Till you/Can read these signs/Burma-Shave."

Gramps and his first wife, Elizabeth, had three kids while living in Japan—Dick, Tootsie, and Dot—my mom. Sadly, Elizabeth died at a fairly young age from cancer. Sometime later, Gramps married Grammie, and they had four more children—Gigi, Gerald, Janine, and Lauren–quite literally the movie star side of our family who had starred in movies, theater, and television! Gigi has a star on the Hollywood Walk of Fame. My sisters and I had been told Grammie and Gramps were very wealthy as owners of a hotel and motel in "Sin City" Las Vegas. Mom always sewed us new clothes for the trip so we would look perfect. Grammie was like our guardian angel and got us those big Easter baskets with cellophane over the top filled with chocolate eggs, tasty yellow chicks, white marshmallow bunnies, and a little stuffed animal. Mom and Dad couldn't afford luxuries such as that. Gramps *always* gave each of us a silver dollar every time we visited. It made every Easter magical.

But getting to Las Vegas was a six-hour drive with us four kids squeezed together like sardines in the back of the '56 Ford wagon, or '61 Fleetwood Cadillac Dad had purchased from Gramps (who bought a new Caddy about every four years). The Ford wagon looked cool, a ranch wagon with steer heads embossed into the top of the two-toned beige bench seats. The Caddy was a light sea-foam green with vinyl tuck-and-roll style seats. It had big fins on the back quarter panels, every option available, and special Vogue tires Gramps always put on his Caddy's when he drove them off the showroom floor in Las Vegas. Dad would *never* turn on the air conditioning, even though it worked perfectly. It was sticky and sweaty and icky in the backseat for sure.

"You're touching me! Stop touching me!"

"No, I'm not!"

"Yes, you are!"

Which only stopped when Mom reached over the front seat with a hairbrush or other weapon in her left hand and started smacking every kid in reach until we would shut up. I was no dummy; I sat directly behind Mom against the rear side window. It was physically impossible for her to reach me with the hairbrush in that strategic position. Like the high ground in a battle, I had the best location to observe the chaos to the left of me and laugh at the plight of my "sisty-uglers."

In 1958 at eight years old, I was put into Cub Scouts. That same year Dad became an umpire and put me in Little League baseball playing for the

John Wayne Dukes. I had no idea who John Wayne was, but I do know he showed up in person to pump us up! I had a pleather fielder's glove–not plastic, not leather, pleather. The coach threw me a fastball to see if I could catch it. When the ball hit the glove, the stitching holding it together snapped and the fingers of the glove looked like a five-fingered gardening glove instead of a baseball glove.

The coach immediately shouted, "Hey, Sam! Have we still got that old catcher's mitt in the equipment bag?"

Sam checked and yelled back, "Sure do, Coach!"

He bent down, looked me in the eye, and said, "Son, you're our new catcher."

They turned me into an All-Star catcher over the next three years. That's the good news. The bad news was my oversized Frankenstein head was too big for the helmets every team got from the league, so the coach had to take the liner out of one helmet so I could protect my head while batting. Every time I swung hard the liner-less helmet spun around on my head like a top and fell off. It made me feel like a total jerk, and I hated to go to bat. Then one day I forgot to put on my catcher's cup and I got a foul tip into my "family jewels."

After five minutes rolling in the dirt, holding my crotch while groaning and moaning like a dying man, they pulled me onto my feet and said, "Walk it off, Son. Walk it off!"

That short walk to the dugout was the longest walk I've ever taken in my life with my teammates snickering and doing fake moans and holding their 'privates' while mocking me. You can "bet your bippy" I never forgot to wear my catcher's cup again!

LK played for different team and had powered two homeruns right out of the park. As my best friend, he convinced his pitcher buddy to toss me a slow "cream puff" right into my power zone, hoping I could hit at least one home run during my Little League career. I hit it to the wall in deepest center, but it was caught in front of the scoreboard. LK: 2, Biff: 0 on Little League homeruns.

In 1959 at nine years old baseball, and the Los Angeles Dodgers were my life. My grampie in Mitchell listened intently to every Dodger game while rocking in his rocking chair, pausing only occasionally to spit into his spittoon or "hit the head."

My uncle Pee Wee sat in his screened in front porch on Main Street in Mitchell with the Dodger game blaring, waving at every passerby. As a mailman, he knew everybody on his route, and they knew and loved him. I spent many a summer night with him, his wife, Aunt Janice, and cousins' Barry and Terri.

In 1959, the Los Angeles Dodgers won the World Series over the Chicago White Sox 4 games to 2. The inimitable Vin Scully and Jerry Doggett announced the games on KMPC 710. The Dodgers played in the Los Angeles Memorial Coliseum, where Wally Moon could hit his metal screen "moon shots" to left field to thrill the fans. Walt Alston was the manager. My favorite players to fill the diamond were Duke Snider in right field, Don Demeter in centerfield, Wally Moon in left field, Jim Gilliam at third base, Maury Wills at shortstop and stealing bases, Charlie Neal at second base, Gil Hodges at first base, Johnny Roseboro at catcher, and pitchers Don Drysdale, Sandy Koufax, and Johnny Podres, with Larry Sherry in relief. I had all their baseball cards, knew all their stats, and spread their cards out on my parents' bed every game listening to the play-by-play. I hardly ever missed a game that year.

My dad miraculously got me a home run ball signed by Duke Snider to go with my black Duke Snider bat. Dad became my instant hero, larger than life. He took me to my first Dodger baseball game in the Coliseum and plopped me down with an adult-sized Dodger hat, Dodger dog, bag of peanuts, and a frozen chocolate malt. He knew I'd polish off the Dodger dog and the peanuts quickly, and that it would take me seven innings to eat the frozen chocolate malt with that tiny wooden spoon they gave you. By the seventh inning stretch, I had finished the malt, and Dad was ready to leave to avoid the horrendous traffic jam that would surely develop if we left at the end of the game. I was to learn from going to future Dodger games with him in Chavez Ravine that it didn't matter if the game was a nail-biter or a groaner, he always left at the seventh inning stretch.

Aunt Janice and Terri both had the same sweet smile and great sense of humor. Barry and I became buds; we traded my shoebox full of Topps baseball cards with Bazooka bubble gum back and forth too many times to remember, but always for a dollar—a measly buck for Mickey Mantle, Willie Mays, Duke Snider, Sandy Koufax, Don Drysdale, Maury Wills, and other famous baseball stars that today are worth thousands of dollars! What do kids care about the value of paper cards when there's a yellow Helms Donut Truck out front with dozens of donuts to choose from? The driver would pull out those super long trays so you could see all the donuts, smell the donut air, and pick to your heart's content. It just doesn't get any better for a kid than devouring a few scrumptious Helm's donuts under a shade tree on a bright, sunny summer morning, and then washing it down with a slosh from the garden hose.

Fast forward to fourteen years old in Van Nuys, California. I was riding my black Huffy three-speed on Burbank Boulevard near Kester Avenue when it seemed like the Hand of God pushed my big Frankenstein head (I do wear the largest men's hat size there is) hard left rudder to see this beautiful girl walking down the street in front the Berkshire apartment building. It was kismet, love at first sight, and having a girlfriend was the last thing on my mind as a somewhat normal fourteen-year-old boy who had only read Playboy Magazines pilfered from LK's brothers' private under-the-mattress collection. I had three sisters, and had no interest in getting to know more girls *whatsoever!* And suddenly, there she was. I was like a deer in the headlights. I couldn't take my eyes off her. Lauren was tall and slender, and looked like a Roman goddess to me. She had a strong, forceful stride.

When I rode slowly past her on my bike, she glanced quickly at me and kept walking; just like me she had been taught "Never talk to strangers." I have a photographic memory, so my slow ride past her and that quick glance were all I needed to record a life-changing "Kodak moment." I entirely captured her deeply tanned face and high cheekbones, soft green eyes, long auburn hair glistening in the sun, and tall, lanky body that was very prudishly dressed.

I didn't have a clue what just happened to me, just like the Looney Tune cartoons with the skunk Pepe Le Pew who falls madly in love with Penelope Pussycat. My boyish immature mind might wander like a Bedouin *looking* at or kissing other girls until I found her again, but in my heart of hearts I knew she was the one.

Soon thereafter, when I was in ninth grade and she was in eighth at Sherman Oaks Junior High School, Lauren was sitting on a lunch bench with her two girlfriends Vicky and Diane, and a friend named Phil. Lauren looked over into the hash lines and saw me in line in my white, neatly ironed Towncraft JC Penney T-shirt with the sleeves rolled up (no cigarettes or Mom tattoo), white Levi jeans, Hirachi sandals with tire treads on the bottom that LK brought back to me from his summer in Mexico, strawberry blond hair, blue eyes, freckles, and dark lifeguard tan.

She turned to Vicky, pointed me out, and said very matter-of-factly, "I'm going to marry that guy."

They laughed at her and said, "You'll *never* get that guy! He's one of the most popular guys in this school!"

Little did they know she had already won my heart, and it would only be a matter of time until I would beguile her into becoming my girlfriend, my wife, the mother of my children, and the one and only love of my life, dream of my dreams, and sweetheart of my sweethearts.

A short time later, I saw Lauren talking to my friend DA's girlfriend. DA was in the same "gifted" classes as me—he was also, by far, the best athlete in the school. Since we all lived with our parents in houses within a mile of each other, I asked DA if he would ask his girlfriend to set up a "just say hi" meeting for me with her and Lauren near the Berkshire apartment building. He said sure, she said yes, and the next thing I knew I was standing anxiously in front of my dream girl at the corner of Burbank and Kester.

Oh my God, she was everything I'd seen, imagined, and more. Rigor mortis set in I was so shy and nervous. She seemed equally as shy and nervous. Total embarrassment, no phone numbers passed, no date arranged, but fate had cast the die that would soon enough change our lives forever.

When I spent the summers of 1965-1967 as a lifeguard at Spring Mill State Park in Mitchell, my aunt Weta ran the license branch in Mitchell and knew every single person for miles around who had to get or update their driver's license. She was a legend in Mitchell, larger than life, who had a personality bigger than all outdoors and the heart of a lioness. She and her husband were *huge* Mitchell High School fans, and had players from all sports swinging by the house for free food and Big Reds. One such especially gifted athlete TC went on to become a football star at Indiana University who played in the Rose Bowl against the USC Trojans, and then a runner-up for Rookie of the Year on the Baltimore Colts. I lived with Aunt Weta, her husband, Uncle Bear, and their daughter Keta-Kot for three summers.

I called Aunt Weta's husband "Uncle Bear" because in May 1965, when I started my first summer as a lifeguard, Cassius Clay (later known as Muhammed Ali) knocked out Sonny Liston in the first round. Uncle Bear weighed over 300 pounds, stood six-foot six inches tall, and had arms bigger than my legs. I was six-foot three inches and weighed in at 155 pounds sopping wet, and even though I worked out with weights all the time and was very strong, I looked like a butterfly fighting a bear compared to him.

Cassius Clay taunted Sonny Liston before his victorious fight by saying, "I's the butterfly, you's the bear!"

Uncle Bear could have suffocated me like an anaconda crushes a wildebeest, but instead he just wrapped me up until I cried, "Uncle!"

Keta-Kot was, and is, like a sister to me. She had flaming red hair and was cute as a button. Her friends were cute too. We always got along like a loving brother and sister. I was fifteen and she was a couple years younger so we shared the same love for the Beach Boys' music. She still calls me her FBB–Favorite Beach Boy. I had inherited a good voice and had a base/baritone/tenor/falsetto range that could mimic any singer or group at the time, but coming from California, I loved the Beach Boys. You could hear us belting out Beach Boys tunes together from a mile away in the second house on the hill.

One summer day after church, the whole family had a picnic in Pioneer Village at Spring Mill State Park. Sunday always began at Jacob Finger United Methodist Church in Mitchell. I was just a kid, but I loved going to that church! We had our own family pews, we sang hymns, we attended church school where they served cookies and milk, and my crush, Kathy, was usually there.

After church services and school, we'd head over to Greek's on Main Street for vanilla or cherry sodas and snacks–what an absolute treat to me. I was a 'bottomless pit', so on the way to Spring Mill State Park for our family picnic we'd stop at Ted's for a breaded and grilled pork tenderloin. I was quite literally in hog heaven.

The picnics in Pioneer Village were always a blast. Aunt Ruth always brought her delicious fried chicken. Uncle Bear dropped a whole watermelon in the ice-cold brook to serve up later. Aunt Weta made all kinds of goodies. Uncle Barnes, a professional photographer, took pictures. Uncle Bub and Aunt Jenny Rose played badminton. Uncle Henie and Aunt Penny played croquet. Uncle Pee Wee and Aunt Janice threw the frisbee. My cousins Larry, Judy, Darwin, Ken, Randy, Barry, Terri, Jeff, Kathy, Jay, Holly, and Keta-Kot chased each other around or played lawn darts or cornhole or horseshoes or Hide-and-Seek or Red Rover. We swung on the swings or slid down the giant steel slide (unless it was in the sun and so hot it would peel the skin off our legs!). We played baseball with a huge plastic bat and a whiffle ball.

One time Keta-Kot and I were chasing each other around when she accidentally fell. I went back to pick her up but heard the thundering feet of Uncle Bear charging toward me like a freight train, eyes blazing with anger, determined to punish me for knocking his precious daughter to the ground. I thought he was going to kill me first, and ask questions later, so I "skedaddled" out of there like a rabbit chased by a fox.

Keta-Kot was screaming at the top of her lungs, "Daddy! Daddy! Stop, I'm okay! It was an accident!"

But the Bear just kept a comin', and I ran for the hills. His big paw ran down my T-shirt as I escaped, but he couldn't grab it, so I was off like a bolt of lightning and free. He picked Keta-Kot up, made sure she was safe and sound, and I came back to the picnic site. We played other no-contact sports for the rest of the picnic.

I didn't start dating Lauren until after I came back from a summer in Mitchell at age sixteen in 1966. In the summers of 1965 and 1966, before I dated Lauren, some very cute Mitchell girls allowed me to give them a kiss or two. Hey, all the other lifeguards were kissing their girlfriends, so why not me? Jill lived right across the alley from Aunt Weta's first house (the one where we ran down the alley in the fog behind the mosquito repellent machine like a bunch of morons), Pam lived a few houses down from Uncle Bub and Aunt Jenny Rose's house across from the middle school, and Debbie lived on the same street as Pam a few doors down. My favorite of all was Susi, who lived down the hill from Aunt Weta's second house.

Jill would only allow me to kiss her on Saturday afternoons, when she was wearing her giant curlers, getting ready for the Saturday night dance at the Armory in Bedford, Indiana. We first had to ride our bikes for two miles out to Spring Mill State Park on the secret back road. Then we'd sit on a log and she let me kiss her until she got tired of me. Then we'd ride back on our bikes to Mitchell. Not terribly romantic, but she was a great kisser, so whenever she snapped her fingers, I'd come a runnin' across the alley.

Pam would only let me kiss her very politely on her parent's front porch. I heard she had a boyfriend she'd temporarily broken up with, so I'm pretty sure I was being used to make him jealous so she could get him back. No matter, a kiss is but a kiss; she was totally cute and out of my league, and being used or not, I willingly complied. She was only a few houses down from my uncle Bub, Aunt Jenny Rose, and their kids Darwin, Ken, and Randy's house so I always had a good excuse to skootch down to Pam's for a kiss or two if she was so inclined.

I met Debbie through Aunt Weta. I was told she had broken up with her boyfriend recently and was a "really sweet girl." She truly was pretty and funny and an absolute delight to be with. We drove around one night in Aunt Weta's fast and furious '64 metallic blue Pontiac Catalina for hours trying to find someplace to make out, but everywhere we went somebody showed up, including a Mitchell policeman.

Uncle Bear had offered me his '56 flathead Ford V-8 with "three on the tree" that had an amazing exhaust system and was great for driving down to the pool hall on Main Street to play snooker with the guys, but it was no romantic match for the comfy front bench seat in the Catalina. Debbie and I kissed as much as we could between laughing at our unbelievable predicament, and regretfully I took her home.

Susi was my all-time favorite. The consummate tom-boy and girl next door, always happy, always joyful and fun-loving, always up for sports. She knew her own mind and would hug me and kiss me whenever *she* felt like it. A truly liberated young woman. I liked her *very* much, and totally enjoyed spending time with her. I knew I would be going back to California after the summer and didn't want to lead her on or hurt her feelings. In my mind, I wanted to kiss a lot of girls, but in my heart of hearts I already knew Lauren was the one, even though we hadn't even had our first date yet. I guess that's what love at first sight and true love look like in real life. I was going to find Lauren and make her "mine."

The summer of 1967 was my last as a lifeguard at Spring Mill State Park. We five lifeguards averaged seven saves per person, meaning we had to jump into the icy cold water seven times to rescue a drowning park visitor. Fortunately, nobody drowned under our watch (which did happen in other places nearby). We did have other duties when attendance was low. We picked up trash around the park with a stick that had a nail at the end. We tossed chlorine tablets into the swimming area when the goopy green mossy stuff built up too heavily. We killed copperheads and water moccasins that liked to live in the bulrushes at the end of the swimming area. I learned to do a whole bunch of fancy dives off the pier's diving board, showing off all my diving skills while all the park visitors were beached every two hours for a mandatory break. I nearly got accidentally choked to death and drowned by Mitchell's star athlete turned lifeguard DD goofing around on a break.

If his beautiful girlfriend, Brenda, hadn't screamed, "Stop! You're choking him to death!" I'd have been pushing up daisies in Mitchell cemetery. DD was a jokester, just like me; a total hoot, and my Mitchell Bro-Mo.

One Saturday night, my buddies dragged me over to the Bedford Armory for the usual summer Saturday night dance. Before the dance, they pulled over in the dark behind an old abandoned gas station and dragged out beer and whisky to make "Boilermakers." I'd heard the term before, but didn't have a clue what it was. Well, three Boilermakers later, I knew the answer to that riddle. I remember driving off in the shotgun seat toward the Armory. I remember waking up on my back like an upside-down beetle dancing to the music with a whole bunch of people looking down at me. Fade out.

Fade back in, I remember being pushed out of the car at Aunt Weta's house like a sack of dirty laundry. And I remember being looked at with disgust after that by every nice girl in Mitchell for being a drunken bum. Oh well, *c'est la vie*, I'd be back in California soon anyway trying to relocate the love of my life.

Just before heading back for California, another lifeguard introduced me to a local girl named Charlotte who came to our beach about once a week with her girlfriends. She said she had a boyfriend in Bedford, and I told her I had a girlfriend in California, so we just talked about the things teenagers usually talked about.

My Indiana-born dad's last parting words to me when I left to go lifeguard at Spring Mill that summer were, "Keep it in the holster, Son—no shotgun weddings."

I was a bit puzzled by that remark, but I listened to his advice, nodded, and took it to heart. Boy was he right!

It turned out that Charlotte hated small town America, resented her boyfriend for going away for the summer to Florida to stay with his grandparents, and wanted to live in California in the worst way. One afternoon, she stayed late at the beach after her girlfriends left and innocently asked me if I could drop her off at her grandparents' house on my way home when my shift ended at five P.M.

"Sure, why not?"

We stopped at a big, old white two-story house with a wide front porch, black trim, and her own private outside entrance to the basement her grandparents had fixed up for her.

"C'mon in. I want you to meet my grandparents. They're really nice. It'll only take a few minutes and you can be on your way."

I stepped inside with her, plopped myself down on a big, comfy couch, and took a little 'snoozer' while waiting for her grandparents to come down. The next thing I knew she was tapping me on the shoulder and standing in front of me naked as a jay bird looking like an in-the-flesh Playboy centerfold. I was dumbfounded.

She bent over, looked deep into my eyes, and purred, "I want to go back to California with you and marry you. And I want Lauren to sit in the front row and watch the wedding." Then she took my face in her hands, and planted a big French kiss on my lips.

Suddenly, Robbie the robot from Space Family Robinson flashed before my eyes. "Danger, Will Robinson. Danger!"

I pulled away with my dad's warning piercing my now bloodless brain, leaped up, ran out the door, and raced for the car.

In the background she was screaming, "I'm gonna tell my boyfriend you raped me! He's gonna kill you!"

I peeled out of there like a NASCAR stunt driver, sending burning rubber and gravel in every direction. I never looked back, never went back, and thank goodness her boyfriend never came back to kill me.

Being the moronic virgin teenage boy that I was, I made the mistake of writing a letter to Lauren about Charlotte's lustful desire for me, thinking, surely, she would see what a 'great catch' I was. A pinch of jealousy is a good thing, right? As Bugs Bunny used to say, "What a muh-roon! What an ig-nor-animus! What a tah-rah-rah-goon-deay!" Or something to that effect. *Never* get a woman with a Spanish temper angry—never!

She wrote back, *Drop dead!*

Gee, what a surprise! Thank goodness she already understood how goofy I was, and that I "couldn't find it with both hands" as the expression goes.

When I got back to California, she forgave me for my trespasses, and even let me take her to my high school graduation prom. Lauren was the belle of the ball, the stars were shining in the heavens, and I was the happiest young man in the whole wide world.

Chapter Two
Young Adulthood

In California, as a boy turning into a man, there were four adults who shaped my young adulthood. My dad, Bill, my mom, Dot, my aunt Helen—Dad's sister, and my uncle Red—Aunt Helen's husband. Even as a little kid and young man, I loved them all, appreciated them all, and knew they always had my best interests at heart. I have never blamed, nor will I ever blame, my parents and relatives for the way I turned out. They did the best they could, and as far as I'm concerned, they did a *fine job* with and for me.

Dad grew up in a family of nine kids on "the wrong side of the tracks." Two of the kids died at a very young age—one from illness, the other by a freak automobile accident. He became a high school basketball star, the center on the team that became runner-up in the 1940 Indiana State Finals. He became a college Little All-American basketball player. He attended Indiana University (IU), a top-five basketball college in America, but sacrificed that privilege and honor by transferring to another fine school—Georgetown College in Kentucky—because his best friends didn't have the grades to go to IU. He wanted to become a doctor, but WWII killed that dream. He earned a U.S. Navy medal by valiantly grabbing the gun on his Landing Ship Medium after the real gunner had been killed by a kamikaze attack on the ship. His heroic actions helped save the ship and the lives of the remaining crew. After the war, he met my mom at a USO event, won her heart, and married her. He worked for a major defense company for over thirty years, and became a mid-level executive.

Although we heard he was very extroverted in high school and college, after WWII, he was quiet and introverted at home; always serious. He shunned work parties and events except for the Christmas U.S. Marine Corps "Toys for Tots" toy drives, where we kids got a giant candy cane for Mom and Dad's generous contributions. He became a no-nonsense, workaholic *provider* for his family, having lived through the Great Depression. His outlets were smoking his pipe with cherry-blend tobacco, watching golf on TV, and playing golf with our next-door neighbor Phil, whom he just called "Va-Va-Voom!" Va-Va-Voom was the epitome of Rodney Dangerfield in *Caddyshack*. Dad was a different person with him, like a big kid laughing and back slapping and poking fun. The dad we saw at home was a lot more reserved.

One day, LK, his girlfriend Debby, and I stole one of Dad's old pipes and cleaning kits. We snuck around the corner to Columbus Street and sat on the curb under the streetlight. We cleaned out the old pipe with the pipe scraper, and reamed out the stem with a pipe cleaner, just like I'd seen Dad do a hundred times. We stuffed some pilfered cherry blend tobacco into the pipe, mashed it down with the back end of the pipe bowl scraper, and lit it up, anticipating the wonderful aroma of cherry blend tobacco to envelope us with splendor. Oh my God, the tobacco tasted terrible! The smoke burned our throats, and we couldn't smell a thing with all those nasty side effects. That was the last time we pulled that shenanigan for sure.

Dad did so many kind deeds for me and others when I was growing up. One morning, the Superman version of my father raced into a burning house on the corner to save an old lady from being burnt alive before the fire department arrived. He carried her fragile old body out in his arms to the clapping and shouting of grateful neighbors. He allowed me the privilege of going to Indiana for three summers to be a lifeguard if my grades met the mark. He gave me unwanted "flying lessons" over the hedge and through the willow tree at Aunt Helen's house because I was trying to help him unload the '56 Ford station wagon when he told me he didn't need any help. "No means no!" He was my baseball hero.

One time, he lost his black-out Irish temper and punched a wall with his fist. Then he went into the garage. I went out to the garage and said, "Dad, are you okay?" His hand was shaking like a leaf uncontrollably. I was sure he'd broken his hand.

All he said was, "Son, always remember if you hit a wall, *never* hit the stud."

Pretty sound advice in a bizarre sort of way!

In my college years, I apprenticed under a custodian buddy of mine who taught me how to do professional custom car painting, including candy colors, pearls, flames, pin stripes, and a perfect fade six-color rainbow in acrylic lacquer. My dad let me put up sheet plastic from Standard Brands and paint at least a dozen cars in his garage, including his own. I painted *all* my MOPAR muscle cars in Dad's garage using my Sears' one-horsepower compressor, Binks' #7 spray gun, dual-cartridge Binks' respirator, and exclusively Ditzler acrylic lacquer or acrylic enamel paint.

First, I painted the '68 Barracuda I bought from my mom a bright Saturn yellow and named her "Bananacuda." Next, I painted the '69 Road Runner I bought from my baby sister's boyfriend, Mark, a color named Rally Green (a candy apple green just like the Car of the Year on the Motor Trend cover). It took two gallons of Rally Green paint to get the job done there was so little pigment and so much clear lacquer in the paint to give it that true green candy apple depth and shine.

Finally, I painted my favorite car of all in Dad's garage: my 1968 Dodge Charger R/T. I chose a Cadillac Nottingham Green Firemist Poly, shot a blue pearl over it, loaded on two quarts of clear, and then block-sanded the finish with 600 wet sandpaper. Hours of buffing later, including using corn starch to finish, I called my mom outside for the final inspection. I walked her over to the hood of the Charger and placed a yardstick straight up in the center of the hood.

"Mom, can you tell me how many of the numbers you can read on the yardstick up to thirty-six?"

"Why, Billy, I can read all of them!"

Folks, it just doesn't get any better than that for a custodian turned custom car painter.

Mine was a 1968 Dodge Charger R/T (XS29)—only 426 of them ever built. It had a 426 V-8 with dual quads (two four-barrel carburetors), four on the floor, and a street hemi rated at 425 horsepower (bhp). It had a 156 mile per hour top speed, and could go from zero to sixty miles per hour in 4.8 seconds! I named her "My Honey" after my grammie's favorite car (I considered my grammie a saint to me growing up). It was the fastest car on Van Nuys Boulevard on Wednesday *'cruise'* nights, when everybody who was anybody would circle through the Bob's Big Boy parking lot, drive up Van Nuys Boulevard a few miles racing from stoplight to stoplight, then drive back the other way to Bob's Big Boy, circle through, and do it again. My big sister, Allison, was a car-hop at Bob's for a while. You could park at an angle at the back of Bob's, and a car hop would come to your car on roller skates. She would take your order, then roller skate your food back out to you when it was ready. Sis said she got great tips but couldn't stand the drunken, big-mouthed rich kids from Encino trying to show off driving their mommy's T-Bird or daddy's Mustang.

To set the record straight, the "General Lee" driven in the Dukes of Hazzard TV show was a 1969 Charger. Reports say they used twenty-six Chargers doing the show, many of which were '68 or '70 Chargers modified to make them look like a '69 model.

The '68 Charger 440 Magnum used by the bad guy in the movie *Bullitt* starring Steve McQueen that chased his '68 Mustang 390 GT 2 + 2 fastback *was indeed a '68 Charger* with the same body style and hidden recessed headlights that were on My Honey.

When Lauren and I had our garden wedding at Aunt Helen's house in Tarzana on Easter Sunday, 1972 we drove away in the Charger. When Lauren and I moved to Patrium in late nineties, I shipped my officially antique My Honey over to Patrium to *prove* to everybody that Alkodomo Trading Company had a high level of appreciation for the glory of vintage machines, be they Chargers, Falcons, or Hercs. The R/T was a huge hit with every single person who saw it, and took it for a spin, from the prime minister to the American-born shop mechanic who helped me keep her running like a top. The roads were full of Porches, Mercedes, Ferraris, Lamborghinis, Audis, and Volvos owned by the rich and famous all over the country. There was one and only one '68 Charger R/T in all of Europe.

Dad and Mom offered to help me pay for my college if I was working part-time. I thanked them kindly but said paying for my room and board was more than enough. Right after I got my high school diploma, I got a full-time job working as a custodian for the L.A. City Schools thanks to Mark. I was informed custodians have keys, but janitors do not as a rule. As a high school graduation present from Dad, my very first car was a two-door 1954 Cadillac Coupe Deville, the one with the massive "Mae West" chrome "boobs" on the front. My dad bought the '54 Caddy from Gramps, and Dad loved it so much he had it custom painted with fifty coats of deep copper/bronze acrylic lacquer topped with loads of clear coat. My first dates with Lauren were in that car, and it took us to A&W Root Beer and Denny's and Santa Monica pier dozens of times.

UCLA is a beautiful school set in the hills of Westwood near Belair where lots of the movie stars lived. One semester, just for fun, I went out for the one-meter springboard diving team. I had learned several difficult dives as a life-guard, so why not? To join the team, I had to learn nine dives well, which was a huge challenge for me. I was mediocre at best on nine dives, but at least my mere attendance in any diving meet earned our team a 'point' against the other colleges.

At one meet, our coach started freaking out when our star three-meter board diver got the stomach flu and dropped out. He was frantically looking for a replacement, and there I was looking like a tall, skinny bulls-eye in a tiny speedo swimsuit. He begged me to do my nine one-meter board dives off the three-meter board that day to earn us a point and hopefully win the meet. I thought he had lost his mind. Flubbing a dive off the three-meter springboard is like being smacked with a wet two-by-four, and sounds the same. Imagine doing that nine times for one lousy point.

"There is no 'I' in 'team'," so I said yes. I proceeded to do my nine dives in *terrible* fashion. The judges felt sorry for me and generously gave me all ones and twos instead of all zeros.

The crowd in the stands was actually booing me with every dive until one of my teammates went up to the stands and yelled at them, "Hey, guys, come on, this guy hasn't done a three-meter dive in his life until today. He's just doing it to get us a point. Give him a break for goodness' sake!"

After that, the crowd gave me a standing ovation for every dive I did. Very touching. And then I'd reward them with another terrible dive, water splashing everywhere, never a clean entry.

My worst dive was an "inward one" where I jumped forward, did an in-ward somersault, and entered the water like a toothpick leaning forward—from ten feet off the water—where upon entry the water shoots straight up your legs right into your privates just like being kicked in the groin in a fight. I stayed under water for at least a minute, moaning, groaning, bubbles coming out of my mouth and nose, unable to breathe. Finally, I swam under water to the edge of the pool next to the judges where the exit ladder was located. My head popped up to see five ones blaring in front of my face.

One very nice lady judge whispered, "Son, are you okay?"

I looked up at her sheepishly and said, "I don't know, ma'am, I haven't checked yet." I popped out of the water, got back in line, and waited for my turn.

At the end of the day, we won the meet, and I quit the diving team forever.

I have asked many men and women with military backgrounds this question, including my dad: "What is the best and shortest way to describe a man or woman who you totally admire and respect, who has demonstrated time and time again the qualities of integrity, honesty, trust, and caring? Someone you love as a person, and human being, but with whom you may not want to use the word 'love'?"

The answer was always the same from Dad and every soldier, sailor, airman, Marine, or Coast Guardsman I spoke to. "He's a good man." (Or "She's a good woman.")

Four hours before my dad died, I called him from Patrium halfway around the world to say, "Hi, Padre. Wha cha up to?"—my standard greeting.

Dying in his hospital bed, he softly said, "I love you, Son, and I'm very proud of you."

I said back, "I love you too, Padre. You're a good man."

When I got off the phone I fell apart. We both knew that would be the last time we spoke on this worldly sphere. Four hours later, he crossed over into Spirit peacefully, my mom told me later.

Fast-forward six months when he came to me in a dream. We were sitting at the same kitchen table and nook we'd eaten at a thousand times. I was forty-seven years old. He was thirty-five years old dressed in his favorite tan slacks and green golf shirt and brown hush puppy shoes, the same age he had told me once while puttering around in the garage was the *best age* for a man, because he was old enough to have some wisdom and experience, but young enough to still do whatever needed to be done physically.

So, there we were in the dream, chit-chatting like a couple of fraternity brothers about the sorority ball coming up on Saturday night. And then I woke up. I told my mom about the dream and said, "Don't worry about how old you are when you see Dad in Heaven, Mom. You'll both be exactly the age you want to be. And the version of Dad that's over there is the fun-loving and adventurous Navy captain you dated at USO, and always wanted him to remain!"

We hugged and cried happy tears and took off for Bob's Big Boy where Dad or Mom and I always flipped coins to see who had to pay. Dad always got Pappy Parker's chicken, Mom always got a kiddy hamburger and thick chocolate malt, and I always got a Big Boy, fries, green salad with Bob's Thousand Island dressing, and a cherry-orange coke.

Every single day in my prayers, I say, "Hi, Padre. Wha cha up to?"

And every single day I hear back, "I love you, Son, and I'm very proud of you." Then off he flies into the Heavens to do God's work.

My mom was born in Japan when her dad, my gramps, was working for Harley-Davidson and building Harleys there under license. Just so you know, the first motorcycle ever built in Japan was a Harley-Davidson (see Harry V. Sucher's book). Gramps is in the U.S. Motorcycle Hall of Fame, a few photos down from Evel Knievel. Gramps and his entire family were escorted *hurriedly* and safely out of Japan in 1938 en route to California. Gramps was a very wealthy man, but was not given time to arrange first class passage. The family boarded a cork freighter and away they went. En route, Mom remembered looking out the porthole to see a gigantic wave in the ocean heading their way. Alarm bells were going off as the captain frantically struggled to turn the ship into the wave. He succeeded, they survived, and the freighter kept heading to Los Angeles. The horrifying vision of that gigantic wave has never left her.

When they arrived in Los Angeles, Gramps got a job at a local defense company, and her mom volunteered to work with the USO. My mom met my dad at a USO event when she was only twenty and he was twenty-six. When we were kids, Mom loved sharing Dad's USO Irish black-out temper story. Her mother set my future mom and dad up for a date at a USO dance one night. Dad was wearing his dress Navy whites that made him look like a star in the movie *An Officer and a Gentleman*. Mom wore a beautiful sequined ball-gown that belonged to her mother (who sadly died soon thereafter of cancer). They were having the time of their lives, and romance was in the air.

Suddenly, five drunken sailors crashed the party, swearing obscenities at the other guests, and then my mom. My dad "blew his top," beat all five guys up, and threw them out the front door in a heap. Several guests grabbed my dad to calm him down. After he appeared to them to be "normal" again, they let him go. He promptly raced outside and pummeled all five of them again! Then he came back inside, and calmly sat down as if nothing had happened. When Mom asked him why he went back outside, he told her he honestly had no memory of anything that had happened from the time the drunken sailor cursed her until he sat back down at the table. Hard to believe? You bet. But I can guarantee, from my personal experience, that my inherited black-out Irish temper works exactly like that.

After getting married, Dad was looking for a good job in the Los Angeles area that required a college education. Mom secretly contacted a colleague of Gramp's at a local defense company, and Dad got a phone call, seemingly as a follow-up to the resume he'd submitted to the company. He got interviewed and was hired immediately with his Navy captain credentials working U.S. Navy programs. He worked there for over thirty years and became a mid-level executive. A massive heart attack shortened his career three years before his planned retirement, but he lived through it.

From the time I can remember, my mom was my life. She was with us constantly as children, always taking care of us, always making the best peanut butter and jelly sandwiches in the world. I always looked up to her, then and now. I knew she was very smart, very strong, and very independent. She reminded me of a lioness taking care of her cubs like we saw on TV. After having four kids one year after another, and raising them to teenagers, while my dad worked sixty plus hours a week for years, Mom became a teacher for the L.A. City Schools. She earned a master's degree while working full-time and raising a family and holding a household together. She was amazing! She was also just a tiny bit naïve about young boys.

In my senior year of high school, LK and I played a lot of card games with our school sports buddies. Nickel, dime, quarter, two raise limit of one quarter, dealer calls the game, usually five or six players. We played cards in an empty room in the huge apartment complex behind our house. Poker, five stud, baseball, seven stud, and Black Jack. Nobody got hurt financially. LK and I were lucky and usually won a good chunk of money. I could buy Lauren whatever her little heart desired in the high school hash lines or at A&W Root Beer. I felt like Diamond Jim Brady!

One day, a bunch of us decided to skip sixth period and play cards for money on our kitchen table.

"My mom never comes home from teaching this early," I said.

Well, in she walked through the front door heading for the kitchen.

"Wha do we do?" whispered my friends with fear in their eyes.

I told them to stay calm, don't try to hide the money (I was forbidden from playing cards for money), say, "Hi, Mrs. Child," and keep playing without touching the money.

Mom had dinner to get ready for six people and launched into food preparation, oblivious to us. I scooped up all the money and cards in a nearby grocery bag, and off we went, with Mom none the wiser! Another bullet dodged thanks to Mom's intense focus on getting dinner ready.

All through high school and college, Mom and I talked and debated and shared our thoughts all the time. My dad thought we were arguing, but we weren't. We were *bonding*. This little five-foot five woman would stare up to my six-foot five dad with *no* fear. When she thought she was in the right, she *never* backed down. Watching her stand up to my dad, especially when he had obviously lost his temper, gave me the courage to do the same in my life, to never be intimidated, to stand up for my rights, and always support the underdog.

Surely, my dad taught me to drive myself to my limits, to push pain aside, to work like a dog until I dropped into bed exhausted, and then get up the next day and do it again. Dad taught me to turn my inner dial from a one to a ten in an instant when I needed to in *any* situation.

From my mom, I learned to think, to reason, to measure carefully what I did and what I said, to follow my heart, to be a kind, generous, and caring human being. Mom taught me grace, dignity, and compassion by example. I can, and will, repay her for the loving, caring, and sharing she has shown me every day of my life. I can make her laugh at my hundreds of silly jokes, bring her joy, and show her every day how much I appreciate and love her.

Aunt Helen loved me like a son, and I loved her. She and Uncle Red didn't have any children, so I became their adopted child. As soon as I was old enough to mow their 3/4th acre yard in Tarzana, she and Uncle Red drove to our house every Friday night in their dazzling new white '64 Pontiac Bonneville with a soft, blue fabric interior. Oh, that backseat all to myself was heavenly! No "sisty-uglers" to share it with. They took me to Hamburger Hamlet's for dinner where I could order *any* hamburger I wanted. I got the works with bacon and cheddar cheese and relish and pickles and mustard and onions and special sauce and fries or onion rings and a cherry coke. Then we'd drive to their house in Tarzana about half an hour away and I'd spend the night in a really comfy bed (the same house where Lauren and I held our garden wedding on Easter Sunday in 1972).

On Saturday morning, I'd mow their 3/4th acre only stopping to eat a homegrown pomegranate or plum or peach or cumquat or green bean or ear of corn or tomato or squash. I would watch Uncle Red tinker with his electronics in the garage like a mad scientist. Then they would take me back home on Saturday night.

Aunt Helen came over on every holiday with gifts. She would sit in her favorite chair with her stockings rolled up above her knees and be treated like a queen. She never said an unkind word to me, and was always sweet and kind and supportive to me. She was my favorite "California aunt," just like Aunt Weta was my favorite "Indiana aunt." She gave me some of my most cherished memories of how loving a family can be. Lest we forget her Christmas candy bowl was always full of ribbon candy.

Her husband, Uncle Red, worked for KTTV Channel 11 in a technical role. He had grown up as a farm boy in Kansas, and had more common sense in his pinkie than I had in my whole body.

For example, one day he wanted to move some lumber from his place to Mr. P's place next door. There was only a chain-link fence to separate the two properties. I started carrying the lumber down to the gate at the street to go out the gate, across Mr. P's front lawn, and then through his gate into his backyard.

Uncle Red looked at me quizzically and said, "Why don't you just throw the lumber over the fence?"

Geez Louise, did I feel stupid! From that day forward, I started listening to my intuition instead of my overactive, and often foolish, mind.

I went to see Uncle Red every chance I got when driving between my college classes and my custodian's job. He could fix anything! His garage was full of gizmos and gadgets and whatchamacallits. He was like a mad scientist in the flesh. He made his own beef stew using all his garden vegetables that was absolutely delicious. He brought wisdom and balance and experience to my college studies. He and his pipe imparted a grand sense of intelligence and philosophy. I thought he was the sagest man I ever met, a combination of Will Rogers and Mark Twain, which is just what I wanted to grow up to be! He taught me fancy degrees and years of college education can't hold a candle to common sense, wisdom, experience, and the ability to think clearly without malice or prejudice. I admired and respected Uncle Red like no other man I'd ever met. He was indeed "a good man."

With this wealth of human talent surrounding me, I began my senior year in high school. As a sixteen-year-old senior in high school, I was in an eight-person madrigal group called the "Vannaires." Four boys, four girls, and our teacher Mr. G. My older sister, Allison, was also in the group. We sang at school functions and did plays like *Frankie & Johnny*. The guys sang as a barber shop quartet at local hospitals and nursing homes—I sang bass.

Since we were "knee high to a grasshopper" my mom had taught us four kids to sing "Bless This House" with her every Thanksgiving, a family tradition all the relatives loved to hear on our clunky black phone in Indiana. I could sing like a bird, but could only read music one note at a time. I could never get the hang of sight-reading music even after a year of taking piano from my mom and learning to play "Clouds." She could play "Flight of the Bumblebee," so you know she was good. She thought I was sight reading the music sheets, but I had really just memorized the song note by note when she was away teaching school. When she handed me my next song and I couldn't sight read it, the jig was up. She gave me a choice: play outside from now on or take more piano lessons. Like any selfish lad, I chose the former; a choice I regretted many a time.

I was chosen as the male lead by Mr. G for *Frankie & Johnny*, a big surprise for a tall, skinny kid who just once got called "Ichabod Crane." When we were in the auditorium practicing, I heard this angelic voice belting out "Marry me, marry me" at the back of the auditorium. If I'm lying, I'm dying, it was Lauren practicing one of her lines in *The Music Man* for the school choir. It was like Zeus had struck me with a bolt of lightning. There she was again, the girl of my dreams; I'd found her again! I instantly vowed track her down in choir, and tried to use my star power as the lead in the play to win her heart. True love conquers all, right? And, c'mon, I was the *lead*!

On the way home that day, I was riding in the back of a station wagon driven by my buddy's mom. Once again, kismet turned my head to the left, and there she was. Lauren was walking as fast as she could down the sidewalk, looking like she was late for her bus.

I yelled over, "Hey, Lauren, would you like a ride home with my buddy's mom?"

She squinted and yelled back, "I don't take rides from strangers!"

Oh my God, what the heck? I'm not a stranger! We met just last year on the corner of Burbank and Kester! Okay, I've had it, that's the last straw. Now I'm really going to track her down and make she never calls me a stranger again!

The funny part was I found out later she was walking so fast because she really *had* missed her bus. Passing on our free ride meant she had to hoof it on foot over three miles instead of riding with me/us in the station wagon. She was kicking herself the whole way home. Now that's funny!

I did track her down, and I did get permission to ride my bike or drive my mom's '56 two-tone Chevy Nomad wagon over to her parents' apartment across from Van Nuys Park. Since she knew, but I didn't, that her dad had thrown her first friend who was a boy out by the seat of his pants, our first "dates" consisted of walking over to the park and talking while we watched her two brothers play sports, or played some sports ourselves.

Lauren was a definite tom-boy, tough as nails, and could play any sport well. She had beaten up more than one bully, boy or girl, growing up moving place to place like a gypsy with her U.S. Air Force dad, so she had a wicked right cross her dad had taught her. I was star-struck, and loved her spunk and toughness keeping her two brothers in line.

But that's not what drew me to her like a moth to a flame. Her eyes were soft and gentle. Her lips were perfect. Her face was tanned with a flawless complexion. Her voice was soft and demure. We could talk for hours about inner, spiritual things. We both loved driving to A&W for root beers and chocolate-dipped vanilla cones. She loved, respected, and honored her dad as much as I did mine. Her clothes were stylish but very modest. Other guys called her a prude, like it was an insult. As a virgin myself, I considered it a *huge* compliment. She was absolutely, positively, flawless to me.

In high school and college, we went everywhere together. She spent countless hours on the couch at my parents' house just being with the family.

After I skipped B12 so I could be a summer graduate with my older sister, Lauren was two years behind me in school which meant we got to go to two high school proms and grad nights together. She modeled in high school for John Robert Powers, so obviously, she was gorgeous. We were the perfect Ken and Barbie couple, as some people called us.

I began attending UCLA in 1967 seeking a bachelor's degree in history. I lived in my parents' home until I got married. Lauren got her own apartment after high school, worked part-time, and attended college part-time majoring in art history. When I decorated my bedroom in "pirate fashion", including a hand-assembled model of "Old Ironsides," she oil-painted me a picture of a pirate for my bedroom wall. She was a *very* talented artist.

A normal day for me was driving from Van Nuys in the San Fernando Valley, over the hill on Sepulveda Boulevard to Westwood/UCLA, taking classes all day, then driving back over the hill to the other end of the Valley to report to my full-time L.A. City Schools custodial job by three P.M. I'd get off at eleven P.M., drive over to Lauren's apartment in Sherman Oaks for a short visit, then go back home to get some sleep. Same routine working full-time and going to college full-time for four years receiving my B.A. in history in 1971.

College was a time for stupid pranks and idiotic behavior, it seems. One New Year's Eve, my mom and dad decided to go out to a party which they *never* did. Banging pots and pans together at the stroke of midnight was the kind of party animals they had become. Youngest sister, Anne, was only fifteen and didn't have any plans, so she stayed home. Allison, Marcella, and I were definitely ready to "par-tay!" My sisters both made some poor choices and ended up being grounded for a month. I made a far worse choice with LK and we ended up sicker than dogs *and* grounded for a month. We decided to raid his dad's well-stocked liquor cabinet, drink a little bit of about ten different liquors, and then replace what we drank with water. I ended up at home in bed with the room spinning around.

Anne thought I was dying so she called Aunt Helen and Uncle Red to come over immediately (she didn't dare ruin Mom and Dad's evening). That would happen soon enough when they got home with Hell having broken loose with three of their supposedly trustworthy kids. They never went out on a date again until all four of us were out of the house.

A second college-age disaster occurred when DA challenged LK and me to swipe one of our parents' cars for a joyride on a weeknight without them knowing. We figured it was some fraternity hazing stunt for him, but neither of us were interested in joining a fraternity, even though my dad had told me I was an SAE legacy.

I told DA, "Are you crazy, man? Have you seen the size of my dad, or ever watched him punch a wall?"

DA and LK shook hands on this deal from Satan, and then looked at me like I was a chicken. I imagined how terribly this could go, then stuck out my hand like an idiot and joined their pact from Hell.

The two of them actually pulled off their heists and joyrides without being caught, so it was my turn. My mom had a 1956 Chevy Nomad two-tone station wagon that could be started without a key if the car was turned off with the key one notch from the far left setting. I think the three settings were "Lock," "On," and "Start." In any case, I had discovered this secret setting situation while driving her car back and forth to the grocery store or dry-cleaning store running errands for her (I got my driver's license the day I turned sixteen).

After she came home from school, I took her set of keys off its hanging hook by the front door, used the car key to turn the ignition setting from "Lock" to "On," and put the keys back where they belonged. The stage was set. Now all I had to do was sneak out about nine P.M. when Dad was watching TV and Mom was grading papers, have DA and LK help me silently push the car out of the garage and down the driveway, start it up on the street in front of the house, and drive around the neighborhood for a few minutes, turn off the car on the street, and the three of us push it silently back up the driveway and into the garage right where Mom left it. Easy peasy, lemon squeezy, right? I was sweating bullets about getting caught, but the show must go on!

The three of us pushed the car down the driveway onto the street, started her up, and headed for the stop sign at the corner two houses down where our street "T'ed" with another street.

Suddenly, Anne was standing in front of the car, screaming at me to put the car back right now or she was gonna tell Mom and Dad. Unbeknownst to me, she was babysitting at the house directly in front of us where the road "T'ed" and was looking out their front bay window when we were rolling the car out of the garage and onto the street. She knew Mom's two-tone Nomad from a mile away and knew I was up to something when DA and LK showed up out of nowhere. "I promise, I'll go tell Mom and Dad right this second if you don't put that car back this instant!"

I gave the guys my disappointed face, but inside I was doing cartwheels thanking my baby sister for saving me from a fate worse than death if Mom and Dad had caught me. We rolled her back in, I got full credit for a heist and joyride, and never did such a stupid thing ever again.

I promised Lauren we would get married as soon as I got my college degree and had a steady job. I got my degree in 1971, and soon thereafter, Gramps put me to work at his Alkodomo Trading Company as his would-be replacement in four years.

Lauren set about planning our garden wedding at Aunt Helen's ¾ acre home in Tarzana for Easter Sunday April 2nd, 1972. The white vine-covered grape arbor archway would be a regal entryway for the bride and groom. A justice of the peace would perform the wedding ceremony. The spring weather would be perfect, and all the family members would get along with each other in perfect harmony. Well, almost…

Lauren's mom, Marie, came from a large family. Her roots were anchored in the Iberian Peninsula, Spain, and Portugal. She was a gentle woman who loved my jokes and magic shows, and was full of life and passion. She loved me like a son, and I loved her like my own mother. She focused her attention on her two sons and left Lauren to her husband.

Lauren's dad Wally, or "Wall" as he preferred, was a big man with a bigger heart. He served in the U.S Air Force after WWII from 1948-1950 as a sergeant, aircraft observer, and master mechanic. He participated in the Berlin Airlift flying on C-47 Skytrain "Gooney Birds." He repaired and returned-to-flight B-26C Marauders and A-26 Invaders. He could fix any aircraft in the Western World, and this hands-on experience made him a Most Valuable Player to Alkodomo Trading Company (ATC) in Patrium helping us set up their F-16 and C-130 Depot Level Maintenance program with the USAF.

Wall was *extremely* protective of his only daughter, Lauren. Our first dates in early 1967 were limited to walking across the street to Van Nuys Park in broad daylight. We had to be back to the apartment by no later than eight P.M. A month or two later, curfew was extended to 8:30 P.M. By the summer of 1968, we were extended all the way to nine P.M., and could drive to A&W Root Beer together in the '54 Caddy my dad had given me for a high school graduation present the previous year.

One evening we were sitting in my Caddy in front of her parents' apartment talking about spiritual things when the time got away from us. Unbeknownst to us, we'd missed the nine-P.M. curfew. A minute later, her giant dad leaped out of the bushes, reached into car through the open passenger and rear window, and dragged her out of the car like a life-sized Raggedy Ann doll.

"You're late! Don't ever come back!" he bellowed at me.

After he calmed down, she explained everything, I came over the next day to apologize man-to-man, and he allowed me to take her on another date. I knew the big guy liked me, and I sure liked and respected him for the way he protected his daughter.

All was good until one summer evening when Wall and Marie went out on a date and left Lauren's older brother in charge. Our curfew was nine P.M., and we were sitting on the front porch stoop of the apartment on time. Big brother wanted her *inside* the apartment at nine P.M., not sitting outside, which apparently "didn't count" for getting home on time. When she told him to buzz off, he came back out with a bucket of water and poured it over *my* head! I remember leaping up and chasing him inside, him pulling a rifle off his bedroom wall and yelling, "I'm going to kill you!" I remember grabbing his curly hair with my left hand, and punching his head with my right hand in his bedroom. I remember waking up fifteen steps away in the living room still punching his head. I threw him to the side violently and started out the front door. He had stumbled into the TV on the aluminum TV stand which fell into the wall. Result: a broken TV and a hole in the wall that I got blamed for.

When Wall and Marie got home and saw the damage, he asked both kids what had happened. Big brother blamed me for the damage, and his sister for not coming into the apartment on time. She told the whole truth and nothing but, including him pulling the rifle off the wall and saying he was going to kill me. She blamed big brother for the whole incident, and for overreacting unnecessarily.

Her dad was upset about his favorite TV being broken, the hole in the wall he'd have to repair, and Lauren not defending her brother more vigorously (blood is thicker than water). I was forbidden from ever coming over to see Lauren again.

The next morning, Lauren confirmed her dad was home, so I skedaddled over in my car to catch him. He was standing inside at the front door looking down on me. I was looking up at him from below, handicapped by a two-foot front porch stoop, so he looked like the wrestler Andre the Giant from my vantage point.

He motioned me in, looked me in the eye, and said, "I've heard the whole story. Yes, you will get me a new TV. I'll fix the hole in the wall. If you can do this, I'll let you keep dating my daughter. If you can't, you're done here." He proceeded to lie down on the ground, grab the end of the leg of one of their heavy wooden kitchen table chairs, and lift all four legs off the floor with one hand/leg. A barroom magic trick if there ever was one. Then he put it down. "Your turn," he said.

I lay down on the floor, tried to do what he'd just done, and my puny wrist buckled with only one leg off the floor. *Oh man, this isn't looking good for the kid*, I thought. Thinking fast, I remembered a stunt my former U.S. Army Colonel Uncle Dick had taught me that nobody else in my family, nor any of my buddies, could do. I said, "Sir, I can't do what you just did. But I can do this. Can you?"

I stood up totally straight at attention, put my right leg straight in front of my body at a ninety-degree angle, dropped my body all the way down to the floor on my left knee, held the position with my hands at my sides, came straight back up, put my right leg back down next to my left leg, returned to standing up totally straight at attention, and saluted just like Uncle Dick had taught me.

He chuckled with a smile on his face, stroked his chin, shook his head slowly, waved me toward the front door with the back of his hand, and said, "Lauren will be ready for your date at seven. She has some potatoes that need to be peeled first."

I knew then and there in my heart of hearts her dad had accepted me into the family, he trusted me to take care of his daughter just like he had, and I truly loved her. The baton was passed from father to future son-in-law. That was the day this boy became a man.

Chapter Three
My Path to Patrium

For three generations, my family has been rooted in the U.S. aerospace, defense, and aviation industries. In 1939, my grandfather, Alfred Perreau, joined a major Southern California (SoCal) aerospace defense company. Many of the major U.S. aerospace defense companies had brick-and-mortar operations in SoCal. When his employer discovered that from 1922 – 1938 he had been Harley-Davidson's sales representative in Japan, initially importing and reassembling motorcycles from kits, then managing the first ground-up motorcycle production factory in Japan, and finally building the *first motorcycle ever built in Japan* (a Harley-Davidson under a U.S. Government approved export license), he was quickly pressed into service in Belfast, Ireland in 1941. He led a small team of experts that secretly reassembled Hudson bombers from kits in Belfast, and stealthily transported the fully reassembled aircraft to London, England to use in WWII. After the war, he decided to go into business for himself in Sherman Oaks, California, and named his company Alkodomo Trading Company.

My father, Bill Child, worked for the same defense company as Gramps for thirty years from 1953-1983. He retired as the materiel program manager for the Navy P-3C aircraft. Dad had served with the U.S. Navy in WWII aboard USS LSM-214 (Landing Ship Medium) and was assigned to the Asiatic-Pacific theatre during the Okinawa Gunto Operation in 1945.

I joined my grandfather's Alkodomo Trading Company right out of UCLA in 1971. Gramps had formed Alkodomo Trading Company in 1945, and by 1971, when I graduated from college, had over one hundred clients in twenty countries around the world. He had well-established and highly profitable customer relationships in Japan, Australia, South Korea, Thailand, England, Ireland, Scotland, Sweden, Norway, Finland, France, Austria, Belgium, the Netherlands, Switzerland, Spain, Portugal, Poland, Czechoslovakia, and Hungary. He was a multi-millionaire and owned both a hotel and a motel in Las Vegas, Nevada with his second wife—my grammie. In a nutshell, Alkodomo Trading Company got very wealthy clients in foreign countries the very best U.S. products that money could buy, products unavailable to them in their country of origin. Their wish lists ranged from luxury and high-performance cars to yachts to private jets to wines/champagnes to cosmetics to specialized medical equipment and medicines to designer clothes to furs and jewelry. All completely legal, moral, and ethical. All above the boards. It took Gramps weeks, months, and sometimes years to jump through all the U.S. export hoops and get the desired item to his client. Money was no object. This was all about showing their *status* in their homeland—period—dot. The client was totally responsible for making the necessary arrangements to clear the items through their own national customs agents.

In 1971, Gramps was seventy-one years old, having been born at the turn of the century in Sussex, England in 1900. Without my knowledge for my four years at UCLA, Gramps had been secretly planning to turn the reins of Alkodomo over to me as soon as I graduated. When Dad and Mom drove us to Las Vegas every year for Easter, I spent every minute we were there glued to his side in his magnificent private library. Most of his exquisite books are now in *my* private library. He was a storyteller extraordinaire and reeled in this wide-eyed kid hook, line, and sinker. I listened to him for hours and hours.

My favorite story was how he came to the U.S. from England. His father wanted him to follow in the family tradition and join the Merchant Marines when he turned sixteen, a thought he absolutely hated. The day before his sixteenth birthday he ran away from home with very little money, found his way to London, and got a job as a ship's steward on a charter ship headed for New York City. In those days a ship's steward had one job and one job only—clean up the vomit of any and all passengers who got seasick. That's a full-time job on a transatlantic voyage, but he did it, earned a good salary, and upon his arrival in New York City got a job as an elevator operator in a hotel in Manhattan.

That is an amazing and true story all by itself, but not very colorful by Gramps' standards. It needed some of Gramps' imaginary '64 crayon Crayola box to bring it to life in full color. Gramps only had one arm, his right arm, and only a ten-inch stump for a left arm. He always wore long sleeves, and was constantly flipping his stump around when he took pictures with his Hasselblad camera. Gross! He rested the camera on his stump to steady it, then bellowed, "A little undivided attention please!" Then *click, click, click*. He was a truly gifted photographer to be sure.

When I was about eight years old, I got up the courage one day in the Las Vegas library to ask him why he only had one arm. "What happened to your other arm, Gramps?" I asked innocently.

His eyes twinkled and he told this tale. "On the ship coming over from England, the ship's crew and I loved to play Tug' O' War with a big rope every Saturday afternoon. I had two strong arms to pull with at that age. One day, I wrapped my left arm around the rope *way* too tightly, and started screaming at the top of my lungs when the Tug' O' War began. Alas, the boys on the other side of the rope just kept pulling and pulling until finally they won the contest. When the loose rope fell to the deck, my bloody left arm fell to the deck with it, still twitching and quivering! To stop the bleeding and save my life, the captain of the ship raced over, picked me up, ran to the poop deck, and stuck my bloody stump in a hot bucket of tar. And that's how I got this stump!"

Oh my God, that story gave me nightmares every night until we got back home.

At twelve years old, I told him, in the same private library, I didn't believe that ghastly story, so this time, instead of a Tug' O' War, he told me while he was sleeping on the ship one night coming to New York City, the rats snuck into his quarters and bit off his arm! Once again, the captain raced to his aid and stuck his bloody stump into a hot bucket of tar just like the last tale. More terrible nightmares every night until we returned home.

At fourteen years old, I told him, "Alright. Gramps, no more fairytales, no more buckets of tar, what really happened to your left arm?"

To which he replied that at age thirty-five in Japan he developed a metastatic melanoma on the top of his left hand that wasn't properly diagnosed until a gangrene infection had spread up his left arm just past his elbow. His doctors determined they had to take off his arm above the infection to save his life. He was left with a ten-inch stump for the rest of his life; I finally got the truth!

Gramps and Grammie lived in Las Vegas, but they spent a lot of time in Sherman Oaks visiting my mom and dad. Sherman Oaks was also where Gramps located the corporate headquarters for Alkodomo Trading Company in 1945. In the summer of 1971, I was still living at home with my parents (I would marry Lauren in April 1972). On my first day of work, Gramps sat me down in his Sherman Oaks office and shared his vision of Alkodomo with me. It was definitely a big pill to swallow.

I was a history major at UCLA, majoring in pre-Civil War U.S history, and minoring in post-WWI European history. I had every intention of getting a master's and doctorate in history, and becoming a college-level history professor. Had I known I was to become the chairman of Alkodomo Trading Company after I graduated from college, I might have chosen to become a business major. Not being a very good mind reader, I chose history.

To run and manage his multi-million-dollar private business, Gramps had a staff in place in Sherman Oaks comprised of *only* trusted extended family members. He had told them all for the last four years that his grandson Biff would be coming in to take over the chairman's role from him as soon as he graduated from UCLA. I was welcomed to Alkodomo with open arms and not the slightest bit of animosity. I was family after all, and this was a very successful family owned and operated company that had been in business for twenty-six years.

Danny was the chief executive officer (CEO), the "captain" who ran the entire ship with an iron fist (covered in purple velvet, of course). Her intuition/sixth sense about people and projects was a godsend for Alkodomo. Wanda was the able and trustworthy executive assistant, supported by Doti. Melaney was the chief operating officer (COO) supported by Carolina. Melaney had one of those unique minds that could capture and retain every detail about every item that had been exported to our clients over the last twenty-six years. Shawn was the chief financial officer (CFO), who handled all our domestic and global finances and had kept Alkodomo squeaky clean with the IRS. Leslie was the vice president of exports for all precious jewelry, fine art, exquisite furs, and U.S. designer apparel, footwear, and leather goods—a huge slice of Alkodomo's business. Pia was the vice president of exports for all U.S. made cosmetics, culinary items, and fine wines/champagnes—what a fun job that was! Engin was the vice president of export/import controls and property management—a painstakingly tedious and difficult job that required sheer guts, determination, and infinite patience to accomplish successfully. Godwin was the vice president of exports for medical equipment and specialized medicines supported by Yvette—many of our clients or their families had serious health issues only American technology and pharmaceuticals could rectify. Lee was the vice president of exports for fine automobiles, yachts, and aircraft. Oh man, a business area that was right up my alley! Cadillacs, Lincolns, Jeeps, Teslas, Camaros, Mustangs, Corvettes, Challengers, and Chargers. Lee and I were going to become very close friends working this business area!

Long story short, Gramps spent the next four years grooming his new chairman. We travelled together to every client in twenty countries. He passed along every bit of knowledge, experience, wisdom, and business acumen he could like a father to his grandson. On his seventy-fifth birthday in 1975, he officially retired from Alkodomo and passed the reins to me. Now, he and Grammie could focus on the hotel and motel in Las Vegas which to them wasn't work at all, it just kept them both feeling young and loving life. He eventually sold off the hotel and motel after Grammie died in 1990, at which time he was ninety years old.

In 1995, after twenty years serving as the chairman of Alkodomo, I got interested in what the U.S. government was doing selling used/previously owned and operated U.S. Air Force F-16s and C-130s "out of the boneyard" to U.S. allied foreign governments via the Foreign Military Sales (FMS) process. My long-time clients in Poland, Czechoslovakia (now the Czech Republic), and Hungary were telling me all three of their governments were interested in joining NATO and the EU by 2000. To do so, they would be required to fortify their defense capabilities and buy new or used fighter aircraft such as F-16s, F-18s, French Mirages, or Swedish Gripens. My aerospace roots kicked in and I wanted to learn more. Lee accepted the "tasker" to dive into this new business area and see if there was "a pony in the stable."

Lee 'checked it out' in great detail. He found out that in 1995 aerospace giants Lockheed-Martin and Boeing were actively working to sell new F-16s and F-18s to Poland, The Czech Republic, and Hungary to help them join

NATO. But *nobody* was trying to help Patrium on their quest to do the very same thing by buying *used* USAF F-16s and C-130s.

On my next trip to Central Europe, I decided to make a visit to Patrium and its capital Belgrade. My client in Austria, who loved all things aircraft, got an appointment for me with a mid-level representative in its Ministry of Economy and Trade. You may recall that Patrium is bordered by Italy, Austria, Hungary, Romania, Bulgaria, Greece, and Albania. It was formed in 1992 after the total collapse of the USSR with the signing of the Schonbrunn Peace Treaty. Patrium combined the former Soviet territories of Croatia, Montenegro, Serbia, Slovenia, Bosnia/Herzegovina, and Macedonia into one new, independent, and democratic nation.

The ministry representative confirmed to me the government of Patrium was indeed interested in joining NATO by 2000, was aware of NATO defense requirements, was already spending at least 2% of its GDP on NATO compatible defense related products and services, and had been told by NATO representatives that the acquisition of used USAF F-16s and C-130s would be *perfectly acceptable* to the review committee for new NATO entrants. His strong, no-nonsense affirmation sealed our fate. Alkodomo would be going into the United States Government (USG) Foreign Military Sales (FMS) business with Patrium as our launch customer.

Fortunately, Lee loved the idea. "Are you kidding, boss? Selling used F-16 Fighting Falcon aircraft and used C-130 Hercules aircraft for potential benefit of a U.S. ally, NATO, and the Free World? Count me in!" (Lee was obviously a true American patriot.)

Lee did the necessary research, learned both aircraft in great detail, and delved into the USG FMS sales process. He got Alkodomo qualified as a USG approved vendor for used USAF military aircraft, and by mid-1996 Alkodomo Trading Company was authorized by the USG to sell used USAF F-16 and C-130 aircraft to fully vetted and congressionally approved USG allies straight out of "The Boneyard" at the 309th Aerospace Maintenance and Regeneration Group (AMARG) in Tucson, Arizona located at Davis-Monthan Air Force Base. First stop, Patrium!

In late 1996, I made a second trip back to Belgrade to share the good news. The representative at the Ministry of Economy and Trade I had met with in 1995 just so happened to be the brother of the current minister of economy and trade. After telling my/Lee's story again, the minister/brother immediately walked me down the hallway to see his cousin, the current minister of defense for Patrium. *Batta-bing-batta-boom.* the minister of defense looked me straight in the eye and told me if Alkodomo could get Patrium ten used F-16s, and three used C-130s, and provide 100% offset on the deal just like Poland, the Czech Republic, and Hungary were demanding, *we had a deal.* We shook on it, a gentlemen's agreement, and instantly Alkodomo Trading Company was in the international defense business.

Wow! Lee and I were totally pumped. But what in tarnation did I know about used USAF fighter and transport aircraft? Enter Lauren's dad, the Big Wally, just "Wall" amongst us girls. He had worked on, or flown on, every major USAF aircraft during and after WWII while serving his hitch in the USAF. He had a thriving aircraft restoration business at Van Nuys Airport, totally overhauling vintage aircraft for their final flight to a museum. He could spot and name every single aircraft that flew overhead, or landed at Van Nuys Airport. I loved the guy, and he was an aircraft mechanical genius. And better yet, he was happy to join Alkodomo as our vice president of aircraft operations and maintenance. Lauren, Marie, and I were ecstatic. Wall would be the silver bullet on our F-16/C-130 sale to Patrium. We couldn't have done it without him.

Lee and Wally had the stick on all the USG and technical details. It was up to me to learn the details on what this Industrial Cooperation/Industrial Benefits/Offset was all about.

Chapter Four

The Principles of Offset/ Industrial Cooperation/ Industrial Benefits

There are many allies of the USA that want to buy what they consider to be our best-in-the-world defense articles, products, and services to defend themselves from their enemies. The United States Government (USG) has a well-established Foreign Military Sales (FMS) process for this type of request. Any offset/industrial cooperation/industrial benefits programs that result from these sales are the responsibility of the U.S. prime or independent contractor that produces or sells the new or used defense article itself to the foreign country.

One school of thought says the need to do offset was born back in 1977. The Foreign Corrupt Practices Act of 1977 (FCPA) was enacted for the purpose of making it unlawful to make payments to foreign government officials to assist in obtaining or retaining business. The anti-bribery provisions of the FCPA prohibit any offer, payment, promise to pay, or authorization of the payment of money or anything of value to any person, while knowing that all or a portion of such money or thing of value will be offered, given or promised, directly or indirectly, to a foreign official to influence the foreign official in his or her official capacity, induce the foreign official to do or omit to do an act in violation of his or her lawful duty, or to secure any improper advantage in order to assist in obtaining or retaining business for or with, or directing business to, any person.

It is illegal for U.S. defense companies to use ANY form of bribery, outright or implied, to make a Foreign Military Sale, and VERY stiff penalties apply. The FCPA legislation did *not* apply to foreign governments nor their industry, so it didn't stop competing manufacturers in other countries from using bribes, incentives, and any other means at their disposal to sell their products and services to foreign buyers who couldn't care less about America's FCPA prohibitions.

Besides outright cash payment bribes, other financial incentives our competitors resort to for securing a major contract with a foreign customer include free military or commercial products or services not directly related to the sale, Swiss or foreign secret bank accounts, free travel to exotic places, free college in the U.S. for themselves or their relatives, highly desirable jobs in highly desirable locations for friends and family, free houses/cars/planes/boats, sexual favors, etc.

U.S. defense industry leaders/prime contractors like Lockheed, Boeing, and General Dynamics recognized in 1977 that they needed a way to compete for new international business on equal footing with their foreign competitors. From as far back as the seventies many of the potential international customers for new or used fighter aircraft or military transports were countries that did NOT have enough discretionary defense budget set aside *in advance* to conclude a billion dollar plus acquisition of U.S. defense articles like P-3s, C-130s, F-16s or F-18s. Something legal, moral, and ethical had to be done to counteract the "cheaters" and put U.S. defense companies on equal footing with the defense companies and their sponsoring governments that were competing against them. Call it "offset" or "industrial involvement" or "industrial benefits" the principle is the same. Level the international playing field so that U.S. defense companies can legally compete with foreign defense companies on equal footing. Apply offset to minimize or eliminate any negative balance of trade situation in the customer nation created by the purchase of the U.S. defense article, product, or service.

Offset can be defined as anything of value required by a country purchasing a product or service from another country as partial or full compensation for the purchase. Offset may be required for on both commercial and government purchases. It can take many forms, including but not limited to work placed with local industry, procurement of products or services from local industry or overseas subsidiaries, promoting the growth of export trade, transfer of technology to local industries, training, investments in local industries, and establishing new joint venture companies. Offset must comply with the laws of both the providing and receiving countries. Offset is designed to *enhance* economic growth in the purchasing country.

Offsets are generally classified into two categories; direct or indirect offset. Direct offset is directly related to the end item purchased by the foreign government. Indirect offset includes ALL other activity that does not fall under the category of direct offset.

Examples of direct offset include co-production (fabrication, assembly, and/or testing of parts, components, subassemblies, major assemblies, or final assembly of the product purchased), provision of materials, provision of tooling/manufacturing test/support equipment, provision of training/certification/inspection/other forms of support, provision of opportunities to bid co-production, and co-development (participation in the development of the purchased product).

Examples of indirect offset include technology transfer to the purchasing country, marketing assistance for products produced in the purchasing country, investments in the purchasing country, joint ventures including the formation of new companies with the intent of enhancing economic development in the purchasing country, training in new skills and technologies, procurements of products produced by the purchasing country's industry, concession projects that fulfill a compensation requirement but offset credits are not used to measure performance, and studies/surveys, including feasibility, macroeconomic, depot maintenance and repair, technology need studies, etc. performed for the benefit of the purchasing country.

An offset agreement is executed between a contractor and the offset authority of a foreign government that includes a commitment on the part of the contractor to perform offset in a foreign country. An offset agreement typically includes the offset commitment level, scope/type of acceptable projects, methods of computing offset credits, performance period, performance incentives/priorities including multipliers and/or credit weighting formulas, and performance penalties or best efforts.

The offset authority is the official agency empowered by a government to establish offset requirements and guidelines, and to consummate, monitor, and enforce offset agreements.

Offset credit is a monetary unit of measuring the achievement of offset against an offset obligation. Offset credit is the product of the value of an offset transaction times a multiplier (if any).

An offset credit banking agreement provides for offset credits to be accumulated in *advance* of a contract award, or in *excess* of a fulfilled obligation. "Banked" credits are applied toward the fulfillment of future offset obligations. The "Banking Agreement" is negotiated between a contractor, and the offset authority. Banking agreements encourage the competing contractors to invest time and money *prior to* a competitive contract award.

An offset banking agreement provides benefits to both of the parties to an offset agreement. For the contractor, it provides the ability to bank offset credits prior to the award of a sales contract. It serves as in incentive for the contractor to perform offset projects prior to incurring a formal offset obligation. The benefit to the contractor is the establishment of credibility in its ability and willingness to perform offset projects, and the opportunity to take advantage of beginning projects that have a *time-critical start time*. The ability to bank credits earned in excess of an offset obligation is an incentive for the continuation of offset projects after contractual obligations are met.

Offset banking agreements prior to the award of a sales contract can produce economic benefits for the purchasing country *far in advance of the expenditure of national funds*. An offset banking agreement provides an incentive to a contractor to preform pre-award offset projects, knowing that those credits will be credited to the contractor upon contract award. Furthermore, if more than one contractor is competing for a sales contract, the country benefits can occur from several sources.

An offset multiplier is a negotiated factor used by an offset authority as in incentive to acquire specific offset projects or types of projects that provide the country with *enhanced benefits*.

An offset obligation is the value of a compensation obligation. It is usually expressed as a percentage of the purchase price that a contractor (seller) makes to the offset authority of a purchasing country. It is also called an offset commitment. It is typical for international buying nations to demand a 100% offset commitment.

An offset transaction is any business transaction conducted between a contractor having an offset obligation, and an entity (generally a company) in a foreign country, for which the contractor is awarded offset credit by the offset authority in that country.

An offset "Transaction Credit Document" (TCD) is an official record of each offset project or transaction. It is prepared by the contractor and submitted to the offset authority for processing. Approval for offset is *required* prior to initiating the project.

The value of all or part of an offset project is *mutually agreed upon in writing* by the contractor and the offset authority. The project may be the cash or in-kind-value of an investment, the value of technology being transferred, the value of training provided by the contractor, the amount of license fee or royalty avoided as a result of offset, etc. The amount of offset credit awarded to the contractor is the product of the value of the offset transaction and the offset multiplier (if any). In simple terms, offset credit = the value of an offset transaction X any offset multiplier.

Eligible parties and designated companies must be identified. They are third parties that are often a supplier to the contractor that has incurred an offset obligation. An eligible party is designated by the contractor through the offset agreement as being eligible to conduct offset projects on behalf of the contractor that are to be credited toward the contractor's offset obligation. The offset agreement should include a provision for adding, with the approval of the offset authority, other eligible parties.

The "Period of Performance" is the period within which an offset obligation must be fulfilled. For major procurements of defense products, the period in generally ten years, or the period covered by the contract itself.

Some offset authorities provide *performance incentives* to the contractor to perform offset projects early in the period of performance.

Performance penalties can apply when offset authorities require the contractor provide some form of guarantee (e.g., a corporate guarantee or performance bond) equal to a percentage of an offset obligation. Most countries include a "Good Faith Effort" clause in their offset agreements.

Chapter Five

Setting-Up the Alkodomo
Offset Program for Patrium

In early 1997, the government of Patrium announced the signing of an agreement for industrial cooperation with Alkodomo Trading Company related to the potential acquisition of used USAF F-16 and used USAF C-130 aircraft. The agreement outlined Alkodomo's preliminary plan for performing 100% offset as requested by the Ministry of Economy and Trade (MoE&T). This equated to an approximately $100 million dollar offset program for the acquisition of ten used F-16 aircraft and three used C-130 aircraft by the government of Patrium.

Wallace B. "Biff" Child—Chairman of Alkodomo Trading Company, was announced as the primary contractor point of contact for this potential acquisition.

In conjunction with the signing of the industrial cooperation agreement Alkodomo enlisted the support and sponsorship of the MoE&T in developing its offset program. Biff established a formal Alkodomo office in Belgrade staffed by Dan, Caitlin, and Katie from Sherman Oaks, and consultants Samir and Esmeralda from Croatia. The support of the American Chamber of Commerce (AmCham) in Belgrade was enlisted, and they assigned Monika to help Alkodomo Trading Company (as a U.S. company) develop its offset program for Patrium.

Sadly, in October 1997, my dad died at seventy-five years old in Sherman Oaks while I was on a visit to Patrium. I flew back to Indiana to give his eulogy.

I was, of course, very sad to see him go, but he'd been in such severe pain for so many years after his massive heart attack in 1983 that in one sense it was a blessing for all of us.

In 1998, our in-country team was successful in identifying several new pre-contract award investment, manufacturing, and technology transfer offset projects that were valued at *over $500 million* by our Patrium industry partners *and* the MoE&T. AmCham had provided us with several major U.S. companies that had successful U.S. commercial and military products and services they had *never been able* to sell into Central Europe for one reason or another. The direct support of the Patrium MoE&T coupled with the support of the AmCham headquarters office in Washington D.C had helped them clear *all* the export and import hurdles that had previously stumped them. The Alkodomo team "got the job done."

In 1997, Patrium had established a pre-award offset banking agreement modeling its counterparts in Poland, the Czech Republic, and Hungary. In 1998, after the MoE&T had formally evaluated and validated Alkodomo's pre-award offset projects submitted by its industry, and officially put them "in the bank," word of Alkodomo's success spread like wildfire to the other ministries, and to members of Parliament (MPs). One jubilant MP went so far as to pen a draft private/confidential letter addressed to the U.S. Senate Foreign Relations Committee asking it to consider Wallace B. "Biff" Child as a future U.S. Ambassador to Patrium. Several other MPs jumped on the bandwagon to express their support, with positive emotions riding high on this potential and totally unexpected domestic economy boost associated with the acquisition of defense hardware from the USA that would simultaneously enhance Patrium's chances of being accepted into NATO in the near-term.

One Alkodomo pre-contract award offset project valued at $100 million *all by itself* drew national attention from the moment it was evaluated and approved (and leaked) by the MoE&T. It was in essence a concession project, one single offset project that fulfilled the entire offset obligation of the contractor obviating the need to tally offset credits. Under Soviet rule, Patrium only had one public bus manufacturing company—Marsonia—that built tens of thousands of buses exclusively for use in the USSR over several decades. When the Wall fell and the USSR dissolved, R&D money and export sales for Marsonia totally dried up and disappeared. The new Russian government had no interest in buying Marsonia's dirty, smoky, high-polluting buses any longer when new, clean-burning buses from Swedish and German manufacturers were offered to them for a lower price with attractive warranties. Marsonia had over 5,000 employees on the government unemployment rolls with nothing to do, and no prospects. They were literally "dead in the water."

Marsonia knew how to design and build the now antiquated rigid-bodied, double-decker diesel buses. More modern technology was involved in building articulated buses that were in use all over the rest of Europe for public transportation. Articulated buses were usually single-decker, and comprised two or more rigid sections linked by a pivoting joint (articulation) enclosed by protective bellows inside and outside and a cover plate on the floor. This allowed a longer legal length than rigid-bodied buses, and hence a higher passenger capacity, while still allowing the bus to maneuver adequately.

In the late nineties articulated buses were just coming into fashion in Russia. In many Russian cities that were being modernized, lower railway bridge clearances precluded the use of double-deck vehicles. The U.S. was ahead of the power curve when it came to single-deck articulated buses that were jampacked with the most modern technology in the world. U.S. transport agencies were applying the new "Smart Bus" technology in their buses to count traffic, detect crashes, collect tolls and fares, and manage transit operations and traffic signal systems. So-called "Smart Buses" provided customers with a variety of features, including automated stop announcements, automated vehicle monitoring, and GPS location services. The expansion of data in the "Smart Buses" enabled drivers to re-route around traffic, and passengers to know exactly when their bus would arrive.

Lee and I researched this new technological breakthrough to see if Alkodomo could help Marsonia get back on its feet, recapture its Russian markets, and expand into new markets on the European continent. Lee discovered that the largest "Smart Bus" manufacturer in the U.S. was actively seeking new *foreign markets* to grow its company and make more profits. I knew that Marsonia had 5,000+ employees yearning to get back to work, still had long-established bus buying contacts in Russia, and had the Patrium MoE&T and government squarely behind it. One phone call to the new vice president of International Business Development at the U.S. bus company was all it took to get her on an airplane headed for Patrium with me and Lee to meet with Marsonia management. In the span of one week, Marsonia had nailed down a guarantee for a new $100 million contract with one of their previous Russian buyers premised on the transfer of "Smart Bus" manufacturing technology under license from the U.S. bus company to Marsonia. The Russians wanted nothing to do with going VFR direct to the U.S. bus company. They knew Marsonia, trusted Marsonia, and would only do business with Marsonia.

Three months later, all the necessary paperwork was done, and the U.S. bus company inked the deal with Marsonia under the watchful eyes and beaming smile of the Patrium Minister of Economy and Trade!

The deal was executed and banked under the auspices of Alkodomo's offset program, but since the project made such good business sense it went forward *on its own merits without being contingent* on a contract award to Alkodomo. The MoE&T was incredulous.

My working-level point of contact in the MoE&T pulled me into his small office, closed the door, looked me straight in the eye and said, "Biff, let me get this straight. Are you telling us that this one concession project with Marsonia and the U.S. bus company is truly guaranteed by the Russian buyer to be worth $100 million to the Patrium economy, that it is *not* contingent on a contract award to Alkodomo, and that the project is going forward on its own merits because it's just good business? Am I hearing you correctly, Biff?"

"Yes, sir, you have captured this miracle of perfect timing exactly right."

Chapter Six

Vignettes about Austria, Italy, the Czech Republic, and Switzerland

What do any average Americans know about Europe before you have visited or lived there? Probably not very much. The following vignettes recall some of our most precious moments visiting and vacationing in Europe.

We drove over to Vienna from Budapest to celebrate our twenty-fifth wedding anniversary, visit the famous Schonbrunn Imperial Palace, and soak in ambience that Mozart, Beethoven, and Freud must have felt when they resided there. My favorite color is their so-called "Habsburg yellow" which is proudly displayed on dozens of exquisite buildings throughout the city.

Lauren loves to tell the story of our tour bus ride out to Schonbrunn Palace outside of Vienna. We were staying at the InterContinental Vienna to celebrate our anniversary. The minibar was stocked with two Mozart Chocolate Cream liqueurs "liquid gold" which to "Mr. Tightwad"—me, cost a zillion euros each. Just the gourmet breakfast at the hotel with their world-class chef cost us our whole per diem allotment for the day. Lauren secured several more of the tiny Mozart minibar bottles from the concierge for the long bus ride to make sure we stayed nice and toasty on that freezing April day. A short way into the trip we cracked open two of the precious Mozart vials and did a toast. Her head went back and down the hatch went the liquid gold. My head went back and NOTHING came out! Empty! I'd been robbed! A zillion euros for each tiny bottle and mine was as empty as Scrooge's wallet! Oh, how she laughed and laughed as she handed me another bottle. I swore to get my money back from the concierge which, of course, we did with no problem. That Mozart liqueur "is to die for" for sure on cold, winter day in the snow.

Italy was a relatively short drive from Vienna. We drove to Venice to take a gondola ride on the famous canals, and then drove to Verona to experience the setting of Shakespeare's *Romeo and Juliet*. Our last stop was in Milan, where were treated to special family dinner in a very exclusive restaurant in a precinct of Milan. My Italian-native uncle Ratenni and his wife, Natalia, were our hosts (Uncle Ratenni happened to be the mayor of this precinct). It was like a scene out of *The Godfather*. Just before our meals arrived, a huge man in a black suit stuck his head in the front door and bellowed a command. All the people in the restaurant immediately cleared out like rats leaving a sinking ship!

My uncle calmly whispered to us to "Stay put—everything is fine."

Moments later, about six more men all dressed in black came in and sat down at the table right next to us. I'm a joke teller, so Uncle Ratenni told me to just keep telling jokes, and for Lauren and me to enjoy our lovely meal accompanied by perfectly coupled wines. We were laughing and joking and having a great time which soon came to the attention of the "Men in Black." Before too long, they were craning their necks toward our table to hear the jokes, then passing them down to the folks at the other end.

Finally, Uncle Ratenni stood up, yelled, "Mamma Mia!" and pulled all the tables together family style. We couldn't believe our eyes or ears, but we now had living proof that humor and laughter have *no* national boundaries, and that black is beautiful in Milan, Italy.

In 1997, the Czech Republic came in third in the soccer competition for the FIFA Confederations Cup, a feat they had pursued for years but had never accomplished. We happened to be in capital city Prague for the victory celebration. It was a wild celebration, but in a very safe way. I consider Prague to be the most beautiful city in the world, a storybook land of castles, cobblestone streets, quaint shops, bohemian glass, opera houses, and museums. So many Habsburg yellow buildings as well! In one day, you can take in sunrise on the Charles Bridge, have brunch at Café Savoy, explore Old Town, have lunch at Lokai, tour the Prague Castle, and enjoy a night performance in The State Opera.

Since I was a child growing up in a snowless So-Cal, I had always imagined spending Christmas in Switzerland, surrounded by the snowy Alps, yodeling, cuckoo clocks, Santa Claus, ice skating rinks, ski slopes, and Swiss hot chocolate. The dream came true for the family in Lausanne, Switzerland on Lake Geneva.

A Portuguese friend had referred me to a quaint, family-owned inn near the Hotel Royal Savoy Lausanne. Lauren and I had one room, while our daughters Angela and Claudia had their own room. The inn was resplendent with dark wood, ancient gilding, and European-style Christmas decorations everywhere. There was hot apple cider with cinnamon sticks in the lobby for the guests, whose fragrance wafted throughout the entire inn. On Christmas Eve, they offered all guests the opportunity to take a sleigh ride through the snow to a small nearby church for a non-denominational service given by ministers J-R, John, and Leigh. It was like living inside of a magical Christmas card covered in snow and glitter! When we returned from the church, Christmas dinner was served in a large dining room with a forty-foot ceiling regaled by a giant pine tree covered with live pine cones and old-fashioned lighted beeswax candle holders that hung on each bough. Over one hundred burning candles on a Christmas tree instead of our tiny multi-colored electric Christmas lights? Mesmerizing.

A splendid multi-course meal was served, then the children of the guests were escorted up to the front of the room to receive a Christmas present from Sinter Klaas (Santa Claus) and his black assistant, Zwarte Piet (we had never heard of this distinctly European Christmas tradition).

When recitations from the children were requested, Angela secretly whispered to the Emcee what she wanted for Christmas, and Claudia proceeded to recite the entire "'Twas the Night Before Christmas" story from memory. It was truly a magical and unforgettable Christmas vacation.

The next day we drove to the village of Les Diablerets so Lauren and the kids could proudly say they had learned to ski in Switzerland. The three ski bunnies looked like the cover of a *Travel Switzerland* brochure in their color-coordinated ski outfits, ski boots, and head skis. Lauren posed like the international model she actually was. Angela swooshed down what the Swiss call "nursery slopes" like a pro! Claudia and I struggled just to hold each other up and not teeter over into a snowbank. Then it was time for me to play the role of "lodge hare" and photographer to capture the precious moments, and serve up the Swiss hot chocolate with baby marshmallows.

For our last day in Switzerland, I selected the Hotel Beau-Rivage Palace in Lausanne famous for its winter ice skating rink and igloos. We had an ice-skating rink in our tiny Christmas Village back home, so I had always wanted to do the real thing in Switzerland if I ever got the chance. Ice skate we did, Swiss hot chocolate we did, Christmas carols we did, and so ended our wondrous family Christmas in the fairyland they call Switzerland.

Chapter Seven
The Scandal Breaks

This day began just like any other. Lauren and I were staying in the Belgrade Marriott, as usual, and went downstairs for their magnificent buffet breakfast. The maître de Gabor took us to our usual booth by the window overlooking a beautiful patio surrounded by fresh flowers with a gazebo in the center. Then Gabor handed us the morning paper, and our world suddenly went topsy-turvy.

My photograph was emblazoned on the front page of the newspaper under the words, "The Letter Bomb!" There were photos of me shaking hands with the prime minister, me patting the president on the back, me and Lauren at a costume Halloween party with martinis in our hands and MPs all around us. There were photos of me with the minister of economy and trade signing a supposedly "secret" document in his office in Parliament. There was a copy of "The Letter" with all the "Draft Private/Confidential" markings removed, with a phony date added, and a phony scribbled, undecipherable signature. The article that accompanied all this "yellow journalism" said "The Letter" had actually been signed and sent, and accused the prime minister of being illegally, immorally, and unethically bribed to sign the letter and send it to America so Wallace B. "Biff" Child could become the next U.S. Ambassador to Patrium.

It implied this was just the beginning, a foundation for future bribes and corruption. The prime minister was even pictured in front of the Parliament sitting in the driver's seat of my '68 Dodge Charger R/T with the front door open, surrounded by the president, several ministers, and a crowd of MPs. The implication was he had just been handed the keys to my Charger R/T as a final bribe to "seal the deal."

Based on the evidence presented, the newspaper called on the people of Patrium to *demand* an immediate "no confidence vote" in Parliament, and expel the current government!

Lauren and I were in total shock and bewilderment. How did the press get ahold of the *Draft/Private and Confidential letter* in the first place? Who stole it? Why would they take off the markings and add a phony date and signature? What motivated such a heinous act? Money? Fame? Glory? Power?

Suddenly, all the political unrest that had been in the Patrium news for weeks came back into our consciousness. A national election was on the horizon, and the Communist Party had been using every available means to smear the current government, and convince the populace *they* were the true voice of the people. The foundation of their platform was to join Patrium with the new and rising powerhouse Russia, and turn away from Western influences.

The prime minister took swift and decisive action that very morning. He called a special session of the Parliament to include all the ministers, all the members of Parliament, and all the TV, radio, and news outlets. He asked both of us to attend, seating the president on his right, and seating Lauren and me on his left.

You could have heard a pin drop before he began to speak at precisely eleven A.M. He calmly held the front page of the newspaper in his left hand, and the original *Draft Private/Confidential letter* in his right hand. He faced "The Letter" toward the TV news stations, toward the radio stations, and toward the press so they could get a close look and see for themselves what the original letter looked like. Then his staff passed out copies of the original letter to all with the stern warning they were being entrusted with information that is *Draft/Private and Confidential*, and has national security implications.

He defined the word "draft" as the first or preliminary version of a letter. He defined "private" as not known or intended to be known publicly; secret. He defined "confidential" as intended to be kept secret, private or restricted information. He highlighted the fact the original version of "The Letter" he held in his hand had no date, and no signatures. It was, and still is, a protected government document.

The prime minister squarely faced the editor of the newspaper that printed the article. He stated, although "The Letter" had not yet been sent, it now *surely would be* to show our ally the United States of America how grateful Patrium was for what its U.S. citizen Wallace B. "Biff" Child had already accomplished in this country in conjunction with the potential purchase of used USAF F-16 fighters and used USAF C-130 transports. He stated our ministry of economy and trade, and our business leaders, had evaluated and approved over $500 million in new business opportunities developed by Mr. Child and his Alkodomo Trading Company for Patrium industry on a procurement of only ~ $100 million, a *500% return on investment* for our great nation. Not only would the purchase of these aircraft enhance Patrium's desirability with NATO, it would boost its economy in ways that had never been imagined.

He stated he was honored and privileged to stand at the side of Mr. Child and his wife, and extremely grateful on behalf of Patrium for what Alkodomo Trading Company had accomplished, and could accomplish in the future. He vowed that his administration would work diligently to encourage the USA to appoint Mr. Child as a future U.S. Ambassador to Patrium.

With that comment, the special session of Parliament was immediately adjourned.

That very day the newspaper that printed "The Letter" apologized in writing, on television, and on the radio. It withdrew every unsold copy of that daily newspaper from the shelves. After collecting them, they lit a bonfire and publicly burned the collected newspapers right in front of their corporate office. They never said how they got "The Letter." They never said why they modified it. They never said they did what they did in support of the national Communist Party in an effort to take down the current democratic government. They just turned the page, and moved on.

Chapter Eight
Epilogue

From the time I can remember, there were certain axioms that formed the very foundation of my parents' belief structure, their "spiritual bedrock," if you will. My mom was raised a Catholic. My dad was raised a Methodist. To split the difference, we were raised Episcopalians.

"Dishonesty forfeits divine aid."

"Do things right, and do the right things."

"Nobody can trust a liar, so always tell the truth."

"Love God with all of your heart, soul, and mind; and love your neighbor as yourself."

"Do unto others as you would have them do unto you."

"Always use love all ways."

"Men, just like women, are allowed to cry."

"Be a good boy."

"Respect your elders."

"Always clean up after yourself, and leave a place cleaner than it was when you got there."

"Always protect your sisters."

"Listen to your mother!"

"Always protect the underdog."

"Stand up for your rights."

"No means no."

"We love you, Son."

"Never forget that, in the end, good always triumphs over evil."

The prime minister was a man of his word. He won the next election, and every subsequent election, until he formally retired from government service at the end of his term in 2010. Patrium did buy the used USAF F-16 fighters, and the used USAF C-130 transports. They did join NATO on 1 April 2009 with Adriatic Sea partner nations Albania and Croatia, just before the 2009 Strasbourg-Kehl Summit. And just before he left office in 2010, the prime minister personally welcomed Wallace B. "Biff" Child as the new U.S. Ambassador to Patrium.

SUCCESS

To laugh often and much,
To win the respect of intelligent people and the affection of children,
To earn the appreciation of honest critics and endure the betrayal of false friends,
To appreciate beauty,
To find the best in others,
To leave the world a bit better, whether by a healthy child, a garden patch, a
redeemed social condition,
To know even one life has breathed easier because you have lived.
This is to have succeeded.

Ralph Waldo Emerson

Biography
Steven M. (Steve) Jones

Steve was born in Newark, NJ in 1950. In 1953, his parents moved to Van Nuys, California. His dad went to work for Lockheed-California Company, where he spent thirty years. After bearing and raising four children: Susan, Steve, Laurie, and Chris, his mom became an elementary school teacher for the L.A. City Schools where she spent thirty plus years.

Steve saw the love of his life, Danny, at fourteen years old, married her at twenty-two years old, and had two children, Melaney and Leslie, three and five years later.

Melaney and her husband Lee's son Engin, and Leslie and her husband Shawn's daughter Pia, are both recent college graduates.

Steve put himself through San Fernando Valley State College, UCLA, and California State University – Northridge working full-time as a custodian for the L.A. City Schools while attending college full-time. He taught fifth and sixth grade in Burbank, CA and received tenure in four years. A low salary and weak benefits drove Danny to beg Chris's husband, Mark, to get him a job at Lockheed-California Company, where Mark also worked.

She pleaded, "He talks *all* the time, Mark! Can't you get him a job in sales or something?"

One interview later, Steve got a job in Lockheed's International Trade Development organization, where he learned the "offset" trade from many masters working Canada, Australia, the Netherlands, and Portugal.

Steve spent twenty years at Lockheed working in twenty different countries. He spent eighteen years at Boeing supporting avionics modernization programs, and company interactions with the USAF in the Pentagon in Washington, D.C. Besides working offset programs in seven countries, he supported business development and sales of commercial and military manufacturing capabilities, LIDAR sensors, military sensor systems, cruise missiles, L-1011s, P-3s, F-16s, C-130s, tankers, VIP/SAM aircraft, and helicopters. He retired from Boeing in 2020.